THE VAPES OF WRATH

A NORA BLACK MIDLIFE PSYCHIC MYSTERY
BOOK 8

RENEE GEORGE

The Vapes of Wrath

A Nora Black Midlife Psychic Mystery Book 8

Copyright © 2023 by Renee George

Publisher: Barkside of the Moon Press

Print ISBN: 978-1-947177-48-2

PRAISE FOR RENEE GEORGE

"Sense and Scent Ability by Renee George is a delightfully funny, smart, full of excitement, up-all-night fantastic read! I couldn't put it down. The latest installment in the Paranormal Women's Fiction movement, knocks it out of the park. Do yourself a favor and grab a copy today!"

—— ——ROBYN PETERMAN NYT BESTSELLING
AUTHOR

"I'm loving the Paranormal Women's Fiction genre! Renee George's humor shines when a woman of a certain age sniffs out the bad guy and saves her bestie. Funny, strong female friendships rule!"

—— -- MICHELLE M. PILLOW, NYT & USAT
BESTSELLING AUTHOR

"I smell a winner with Renee George's new book, Sense & Scent Ability! The heroine proves that being over fifty doesn't have to stink, even if her psychic visions do."

"Sense & Scent Ability is everything! Nora Black is sassy, smart, and her smell-o-vision is scent-sational. I can't wait for the next Nora book!

For my husband
Thank you so much for over thirty-three years
of Happy For Now.

ACKNOWLEDGMENTS

A huge thank you to my "you saved my butt once again" crew of BFFs Robbin and Robyn for helping with their constant encouragement to get me to the end. Thank you for being my people! I love you guys!

My husband Steve and my son Taylor for taking up the slack around the house, and most of all, leaving me alone to write! I literally couldn't do this without you.

My BFF Dakota Cassidy for being my one true heart when it comes to all things binge-worthy. I love you, girl!

And finally, to the readers. You are making this midlife writer happier than you can even imagine! Thank you for loving Nora and going on this journey with her and her BFF brigade.

My name is Nora Black, and I'm celebrating my BFFs midlife matrimony!

Gilly is engaged, and I have invited a couple of friends to help us celebrate her bachelorette vacation in wine country. We are leaving work behind for a couple of days of good food, good friends, and good fun.

Or so I thought. When the youngest of our group, Tippy Davenport, gets flirty with a local musician, his girlfriend is less than pleased. Some might even call her reaction homicidal. But when the woman turns up dead during a hiking tour, our vacation turns into an investigation.

It doesn't take a sommelier to sniff out the sour grapes surrounding this murder, including the astringent scents of old money, family intrigue, jealousy, and greed. I'll have to employ my psychic nose to catch a killer and get the bride back home to Garden Cove in time for her wedding.

CHAPTER
ONE

"Oh my gosh," Tippi Davenport exclaimed. "This place has a freaking spiral staircase up to the loft. Can I have that room?"

"Yes," Gilly, Pippa, and I all said simultaneously. I was as adventurous as the next fifty-four-year-old, but there was no way I would be climbing up and down twenty steps of a circular maze every morning and night for the next two and a half days.

There were three other bedrooms in River Bluff House on the Rivière Tranquille Vineyard's property. The vineyard had been established in 1934 by Vigneron Rigel Nichols, a British expatriate who'd stayed in France after World War I to learn the art of winemaking. He relocated to the small Midwest town of Marseille—Missouri; the local pronunciation was Mar-sail, not the French Maa-say—to start his own label. According to the website, the place was still family-owned and operated. I'd booked us a three-day midweek package to celebrate my best friend's upcoming wedding.

After kissing a lot of toads over the years, my BFF Gilly Martin had finally found herself a Dr. Charming. On Saturday, four days from now, she would officially become Gilly Graham. Scott Graham, an emergency room doctor, was the whole package—friendly, handsome, professional, and, most importantly, treated Gilly like a real partner.

I couldn't be happier for her. At least, that was the act I was putting on. Don't get me wrong, I was thrilled for Gilly, and I knew Scott would spend the rest of his life making her happy. Still, I would miss having her next door. I'd moved over to Gilly's neighborhood so that we could spend more time together. But between work, spending most of my free time with my guy Ezra, and consulting on the occasional criminal case with the Garden Cove PD, I'll admit we hadn't seen as much of each other as I'd expected. Still, it had been nice knowing she was there.

I tucked my insecurities away as I gestured at the chunky, comfortable furniture, the hardwood floors, the upgraded kitchen, and the large balcony. I gave a sigh of relief. "The place looks just like its pictures." That wasn't always the case when you booked from a website.

Pippa's blonde ponytail bobbed as she nodded her agreement. "I can't believe I have two whole days without J.J., the dogs, and Jordy. Lord help me, I love them all to pieces, but sometimes a girl needs a few days of no responsibility." Her hips were fuller since having her daughter, but Pippa's delicate bone structure and willowy height made her look rail thin.

"Amen!" Tippi, who was the mini-me for Pippa— same fine bones, same height, and same blonde hair— exclaimed from the loft. "We are wild and carefree."

"Not too wild or carefree," Pippa cautioned her younger sister.

Since moving to Garden Cove two years earlier, Tippi had worked almost full-time as her sister Pippa's nanny. The move and the job had changed the younger woman's life in many ways. For one, she'd gotten and stayed sober.

The irony that we were at a vineyard, and Tippi was our sober buddy, was not lost on me. She'd insisted she could handle it. I hoped for her sake and Pippa's that she was right.

Tippi came back down to the living room. She grabbed her large suitcase and hauled it up the spiral stairs, making me so happy I hadn't been saddled with that space. Tippi was in her mid-thirties and life-cycled daily for exercise. She could handle the impact on her joints better than those of us in the over-40 crowd. Not that I wasn't active. I walked three miles every morning, barring bad weather. Between that and the shots in my knees, I didn't have much trouble. Still, it was better not to add to the wear and tear if I could help it. As my mother used to point out, you only get one body, so it pays to take care of it.

We scoped out the other bedrooms. I was pleased by the scent of crisp pine cleaner and bleach. It meant my smell-o-vision, aka my psychic nose, was less likely to be active. Unless someone had a strong emotional connection to the aroma of cleaning products, I was safe from other people's memories for the moment.

Pippa and I took the two queen suites, and Gilly, as the bride-to-be, took the main king suite. All the bedrooms, including the loft, had private bathrooms, but only Gilly's included a large free-standing tub. It was fine by me. I preferred a shower, anyhow.

"You can see the river from the bathroom," Gilly called out. "The view is spectacular." She slung her arms around me from behind. "It's perfect!" She gave me a conspiratorial look. "Where are you hiding the strippers?"

"I told you. No strippers. It's not that kind of a bachelorette."

"Fine," she huffed. "But I would've ordered you a few strippers." She laughed all the way to her room.

I smiled as I went into my room, unpacked my suitcase, and put my toiletries in my en suite. It was after five, and as the maid of honor, I'd planned this getaway to a T. "We have reservations for dinner at La Sous Terre in an hour. Dress is classy casual."

Pippa popped her head into my room. "Can I just say again how excited I am for a grown-up getaway?"

I grinned. "You can say it as many times as you like."

4

FORTY MINUTES LATER, we were at La Sous Terre. The exterior was a combination of stone and stucco, with a large sweeping roof that gave it a French country vibe. We were dressed to the sevens for the evening and with time to spare before our reservation. Unfortunately, that meant we had to wait at the bar for our table to open. Fortunately, the place had live music from a band called the Ray-tones, and they weren't half bad for a local four-piece cover band.

The lead guitarist, who also doubled as the lead vocalist, crooned Bob Seger's "Night Moves" to five enrapt tables of swaying fans near the small stage area.

Tippi sat on the barstool to my right. She leaned over until our shoulders were touching and muttered, "Hot damn, he's cute."

She wasn't wrong. He was clean-shaven and looked to be in his mid-thirties, but with the chiseled jawline of a high school quarterback. He wore a tight black t-shirt that showed off his muscled arms and chest and even tighter jeans that showed off his other assets.

Two of the five tables were crowded with women wearing black t-shirts with Ray-tones written in fancy lettering on the backs. They were chair dancing as they sang along to his every word. "Looks like he has a fan club. I'm sure they'll let you join." One of the tables had a stack of CDs and t-shirts for sale. "They even have merch if you want to follow him on the road."

Gilly snorted a laugh, and Tippi gave me a sour look. "I just said he was cute."

I fought the grin tugging at my lips. "And you aren't wrong," I conceded. "He's cute."

The bartender, the woman who had checked us in for our house when we arrived, finally came over and took our drink order. Two white wines, one red, and one sparkling grape juice.

"Black, party of four?" a young woman in blue with a white apron asked.

"That's us," I told her.

She held a stack of menus under her arm. "Your table is ready."

"What about the drinks?" Gilly asked.

"I'll stay for them," Tippi offered. "It shouldn't take too long. It's not like we ordered anything complicated. You guys get settled at the table."

"Sounds good." I gave her a grateful smile.

I'd requested a table with a view and was happy when they put us in front of a large window with a view of the vineyard and away from the music. We could still hear it, but it wasn't nearly as loud as at the bar. The delicious scent of sauteed vegetables and roasted meats made my mouth water. Luckily, I'd only had to suppress a few scent-related visions. I'd been working on visualizing walls whenever an unwanted, private memory popped into my head. It helped to some extent, but I still caught the occasional glimpses, and sometimes the emotion behind the memories was too strong to shove away.

"Good evening," the waitress greeted us as we sat down. "I'm Donna, and I'll be your server tonight. Can I start you off with some drinks?"

"We have some wine coming," Gilly said, "but we'd like ice water for everyone as well."

"You got it," Donna remarked. "Ice waters coming up. I'll be back to take your order then."

"Sounds good," I told her. The menus were fancy one-page inserts in leather holders with a four-course selection menu. The appetizers section listed goat cheese and almond-stuffed dates drizzled with burgundy syrup, crab-stuffed grape leaves with champagne butter sauce, and grilled garlic shrimp in a white wine reduction.

"These appetizers sound to die for," Gilly said. "I'm jazzed to try the stuffed dates. It sounds like the perfect blend of savory, tangy, and sweet."

I wasn't a fan of goat cheese. "I think I'll go for the crab-stuffed grape leaves."

Gilly's lower lip jutted slightly. "I wish Ari could've made it."

"She's solidifying her future," I reminded her. Gilly's daughter Ari had been working a summer internship with a colossal cybersecurity firm in Chicago. The girl was whip-smart, a virtual tech savant. "And she's driving home on Friday, so she'll be here for the wedding."

"I know." Gilly sighed. "I just miss her."

I patted Gilly's hand and then glanced over at Pippa. My blonde bestie's brow was knitted in a worried frown. "What's wrong?" I asked her. "Are you missing J.J. and Jordy?"

She shook her head and glanced at the bar where Tippi waited for the drinks. "All this food has alcohol in it," she said.

Gilly put her hand on Pippa's arm. "The alcohol is burned out of the sauces during cooking, but I'm sure they'll leave them off if Tippi is worried."

Pippa raised her brow. "I'm worried Tippi isn't worried enough."

"Do you think she's drinking again?" I asked.

Pippa was a good thirteen years younger than me, but the way she made everyone and everything her responsibility made her seem older. She'd started as my employee and had become one of my best friends. She was the first one I called when I'd decided to open a beauty supply salon in Garden Cove. Three years later, she was my business partner, and our little shop, with online sales and a big client who bought our lotions in bulk, was doing a lucrative business. Her sense of responsibility made her a business asset, but it could get in the way of her enjoying life.

"Tippi is going to make her own choices," I said. "We can hope she makes good ones, but you can't beat yourself up if she doesn't. Those decisions aren't about you."

Pippa sighed as she rubbed the tip of her index

finger along the wood grain on the table. "I know." Her expression was bleak. "She lives in my home, and I trust her with the care of my daughter. For the past two years, she's been in a controlled environment. If she isn't going to a meeting in her free time, she's talking with her sponsor or Jordy. This will be the first time she'll have to face alcohol without a buffer. If she falls off the wagon, I don't know where that leaves us. I love her. I'll continue to love her. But I don't know if I can have her around if she starts drinking again."

I gave my friend a soft smile. "How about we give Tippi the benefit of the doubt until she gives us a reason not to trust her?"

"You're right." Pippa leaned back in her chair. "I'll try to relax."

"You better," Gilly told her. "This is my special getaway, and I don't want any drama."

I'd been so focused on Pippa's worries that I hadn't noticed the music stopped playing until a woman shouted, "I'll kill you!"

We all turned wide-eyed to the bar and saw Tippi getting berated by a short blonde, who was being held back by the band's guitar player.

I glanced at Gilly as the three of us exited our seats. "Drama always seems to find a way," I told her.

She gave me a thin-lipped grimace. "Every. Freaking. Time."

CHAPTER
TWO

There was a collective gasp in the restaurant as the irate blonde threw her drink at Tippi.

Tippi sputtered, her face dripping with whatever had been in the woman's glass. "Are you freaking kidding me?" She dabbed at her cheeks with the back of her hands. Her beige, low-cut silk blouse was splotched with liquid across the chest, and I could see the lace of her bra through the delicate fabric. I took my sweater off and handed it to her. Tippi looked down at her chest and huffed, "This is Saint Laurent. Do you have any idea how much it cost?"

"An expensive top doesn't make you any less of a cheap whore," the woman seethed.

"Calm down, Buttons," the guitar player soothed. "I was just getting some drinks."

I braced myself for the explosion as "Buttons" sputtered, "Don't tell me to calm down." She thrust her hand out, flashing an emerald-cut diamond engagement ring with a halo of smaller diamonds around the stone and on the band. "I saw you give her your number. Don't even act like you didn't."

"Buttons, baby," he cooed. "She was asking me about my rates for a gig." The guy was obviously lying, but I could see the conflict on Buttons' face as to whether she should believe him or not.

Gilly, the peacekeeper, stepped in. "I'm getting married in a couple of weeks, and I have been looking for a band to play at the reception."

Tippi gave her a wide-eyed incredulous look that matched the blonde's expression. She gave a slight headshake but played along. "Yep. That's right. Just needing a band."

"I am so sorry," said the bartender, an attractive woman in her forties, early fifties, with red hair. "Cops are on the way." She gave Buttons a pointed stare. "And you're looking at assault charges for that drink toss. Hope it was worth it."

"You called the police?" Buttons sputtered. "But I'm family."

"Sorry, Darlene," the woman said. "Paying customer trumps deadbeat niece."

Ouch.

Buttons, real name Darlene, winced, then she screwed her face up and reddened. "Uncle Tommy would roll over in his grave to see how you're running this place into the ground. I can't believe he married you. Gold-digging whore," she seethed.

Tippi glowered. "You like to throw around that word, don't you?"

Darlene gave Tippi a once-over. "If the whore shoe fits."

Pippa interrupted, "I don't think we need to involve law enforcement."

"This is a thousand-dollar shirt," Tippi countered.

"That Mom and Dad paid for," Pippa reminded her. "Do we want to deal with filling out a bunch of paperwork at the police station for something that can be fixed with some club soda and a damp towel? This is Gilly's bachelorette getaway."

"Fine." Tippi harrumphed. "I won't press charges." She narrowed her gaze at the blonde. "But Buttons is paying for the dry cleaning."

"I'll do no such thing!" the pert blonde snapped.

"Now, sweetheart," the guitar player soothed. "I'll pay for the dry cleaning."

Tippi, who couldn't help herself, added, "I have his number."

Buttons surged forward with an unholy scream and lunged at Tippi. The guitar player snagged her by the waist and pulled her back.

"You come near my man again, and I'll kill you," she threatened. "I'm not one to be trifled with."

"My gosh, Darlene," a blonde chided from behind

her. "Your jealousy is going to get you neck-deep in a river of crap."

"Mind your business, Ellie," Darlene replied. She turned her attention back to the guitar player. "I swear to God, Blake. This is the last time—" The sirens outside the restaurant and the flash of blue and red lights through the windows brought her up short.

The bartender-aunt waved at Ellie with two fingers. "Get your cousin out of here before she ends up in a drunk tank." To Darlene, she added, "This winery might be a family business, but remember who owns this place. You are here because I allow it, and if you keep pressing me, girl, that allowance will disappear." She brushed her palms together. "Poof," she said. "Gone. Just like I want you right now."

Darlene's gaze narrowed, and she looked ready to explode but, surprisingly, she allowed her cousin Ellie to drag her away without another word. Seconds later, they were out the back door and gone.

"I'm real sorry, Rhonda," Blake said. "You know she didn't mean it."

The redhead shook her head. "Get back to work. Your set break is over."

A tall thin guy with sandy blond hair, whom I recognized as the keyboard player, joined our group at the bar. "Why are the police here?"

"Because your sister can't behave herself," Rhonda told him. "Now, like I told Blake, break is over."

The drummer, a guy with cinnamon-brown curls

and a dark beard, put his hand on the keyboardist's shoulder. "Been waiting on those drinks," he said with forced joviality. "What's taking so long?"

Rhonda popped the top on three beer bottles and pushed them across the bar. The quick move sloshed some of the beer onto the counter. Rhonda shook the liquid from her hand and said, "Here. Now, get back to it."

The scent of beer spun me momentarily as a strong memory took me.

It's dark, but I can hear a hushed giggle as a man whispers, "You're so damned sexy."

"We can't keep doing this," the woman whispers back. "I think he's already suspicious."

I tried to force the memory away, but the emotion behind it was filled with love, longing, and loss.

Cheesily, the man says, "If loving you is wrong, I don't want to be right."

The woman chuckles, then gasps. It's too dark for me to see what they're doing, but her soft moans and his ragged breaths, along with a rhythmic rattle of whatever they are up against, make it fairly obvious. There is a loud clank of glass, then a pop followed by a fizzing sound.

"My beer fell off the shelf," the man hisses.

"Your beer fell off the shelf," the woman agrees, then they both laugh.

I blinked as the memory faded and gave a slight head shake when Gilly arched her brow at me. The whispered voices and the dark room had made it impossible to guess whom the memory had belonged to, and it was just as well, but I had my suspicions. The lead singer had been flirting with Tippi while engaged to Darlene. However, it was none of my business, so I planned to treat it as such.

"Come on, Paul," the guitarist-slash-lead singer said to the blond keyboardist.

Paul looked around the room. "Where did Darlene go?"

"Ellie took her home," Blake told him.

That seemed to mollify Paul. "All right, then." He had a hangdog look about him as he grabbed one of the beers, then turned on his heel and went back to the small stage.

Two uniformed officers entered through the front door and made a beeline to our location.

"Ms. Nichols," the older of the two cops greeted Rhonda. "You called in an assault." He had short dark hair, a little gray at the temples, and was handsome in a George Clooney way. He looked at Tippi and raised his brow. "Is this the perpetrator or the victim?"

The change in Tippi's demeanor with his word choice was noticeable. Her brows knitted together, and her lips thinned into a frown. "I am not a victim."

"What she means," I said, jumping in before it all went sideways, "is that she doesn't want to press charges. It was a misunderstanding that's over now. Right, Tip?"

Tippi rolled her eyes and then nodded. "Right."

"I'm sorry to drag you all down here, Terry," Rhonda said. "Darlene was drunk, and she got out of hand. It's over now."

The officer gave her an aw-shucks smile. "No worries. I don't mind coming out. You call anytime."

The younger cop gave a quick headshake. "Chief, do you want me to take a report?"

Chief Terry nodded to his underling. "I'll get Rhonda's statement. You take one from Miss..." He gazed at Tippi and waited for her to fill in the blank.

"Tippi Davenport," she supplied.

The chief frowned and then scanned the rest of us. "Did you all witness the altercation?"

"Yes," Gilly said. "But it was only some yelling and a tossed drink."

"Only," Tippi scoffed.

Gilly ignored her and continued, "I don't think you have to—"

Chief Terry rolled his hand at the younger officer. "Just get Ms. Davenport's information and record her statement for the report, then make a list of the witnesses' names."

"Is this completely necessary?" I asked. "No one is pressing charges."

"I'll decide what's important," the chief said. He gave me a curious look. "Do I know you?"

Gilly laughed, then muttered, "Well, you do have a type," in my ear.

I elbowed her in the ribs. "I don't believe we've met,"

I told him. "I just have the kind of face that looks familiar."

He smiled. "It's a nice face."

Oh, boy. George Clooney liked to flirt. I shook my head as a smile tugged at my lips. "Thanks." With as much polite friendliness as I could muster, I added, "We were trying to have a celebratory dinner. My friend is getting married in four days." I gestured to Gilly.

"Congratulations, ma'am." The chief dipped his chin to my BFF. "We'll make this as quick and painless as possible so you nice folks can get back to your fun."

Quick and painless amounted to twenty minutes.

"I'm sorry about your evening," Rhonda told us. "You all rented the bluff house, right?"

"Yes, that's us," I answered.

Her eyes were pinched at the corners, and she flashed a smile that resembled a grimace. "Dinner and drinks are on the house, along with the wine and cheese walking tour tomorrow."

"That's generous of you," I said. "But it's not your fault the situation escalated." As a small-business owner, I knew how freebies could add up to a whole lot of nothing.

Tippi's shirt had started to dry, and the alcohol, which turned out to be white wine, was leaving a syrupy ring at the edges of the stain. "I love this shirt," Tippi lamented solemnly.

Before moving to Garden Cove, the younger Davenport had made some serious mistakes. Mistakes that her parents often paid for with trips to the emergency room, occasionally bailing her out of jail for drunk driving, and sending her to several different rehab facilities. They had cut off her allowance years earlier, so she'd clung to the few expensive items of status she still had. This shirt had been one of them.

"Can I get a club soda for her shirt?" I asked Rhonda.

"Sure, honey. Absolutely," the redhead said. She shot fizzy water from a fountain hose nozzle into a clear plastic cup and handed it to me. She pointed at a narrow corridor. "Bathroom is just down the hall. Let me know if the paper towels are low, and I'll get you some more."

"Thanks." I took the club soda and looped my arm in Tippi's. "Let's get that cleaned before the ring is permanent."

Tippi sighed. "Thanks, Nora."

It took some effort to ignore all the emotional memories that could come up in a public restroom. I focused on Tippi's jasmine perfume while I helped her dab the alcohol out of the delicate fabric.

She'd taken the top off so we wouldn't soak her bra with the club soda. Her mouth was set in a grim line, and she looked more upset than when she'd been at the bar.

"Are you okay?" I asked.

"Fine," she said curtly, then shook her head. "I haven't had a drink thrown on me in years, and this is the first time I've been sober when it happened." She gave a dry chuckle. "I should've stayed home with J.J. I'm ruining Gilly's celebration."

"Nah," I told her. "You're not ruining a thing. It's just a glitch, not a catastrophe. Besides, you're a beautiful woman. Someone flirting with you does not constitute a state of emergency."

She averted her gaze. "I might've started the flirting."

"Did you know he was with someone when you started this flirting?" I asked.

"No," she denied. "He wasn't wearing a ring or a shirt that said, 'I'm with crazy'."

I giggled. "My point is, you didn't create the situation or ask for it. And throwing a drink at a stranger because she's talking to your boyfriend has nothing to do with the stranger."

"I know." She dabbed the shirt some more. "I've been the girl who's thrown the drink, and the way Blake was coming on to me, I'm sure he's given her every reason to be jealous. I'm not mad at her about it."

I gave her a sly smile. "That's real grown up of you."

Her expression brightened. "It is."

There was a knock at the door. "It's Rhonda," the bartender said from the other side. I cracked the door open, and she shoved a t-shirt through. "Here. On the house."

"Thank you." I took it and closed the door between us. The shirt was black and had a white outline drawing of a wine bottle, wine glasses, and grapes on the front. It was medium-sized and fit Tippi's slender frame a little loose but not too baggy.

"Cute," I commented.

Tippi looked like she was about to start crying, then suddenly started to laugh instead. "I'll wear this to my next AA meeting," she hooted. "It'll be a big hit when I say my share."

I smiled but asked seriously, "Do you want to have a drink right now?"

Her laughter dried to a halt. "Yes and no. I was fine until that woman threw her wine at me. It took me back to a darker time for a minute. But I'm okay now. Mostly." She looked down at her soiled blouse. "I didn't try to suck the alcohol out of my shirt, so that's progress." She smiled. "Thanks for your help."

"Anytime." I wished I had more wisdom to disperse, but I wasn't an alcoholic. I could imagine how hard it must be for her not to drink, but it wasn't something I'd ever experienced. She didn't have to imagine. For her, the threat of relapse was all too real.

Outside the bathroom, we heard muffled voices. I couldn't make out the words being said, but the tone was distinctly combative. I put my hand on the doorknob, but Tippi rested her fingertips against my forearm, then put one to her lips in a *shhh* gesture.

"What?" I mouthed at her. I was as curious as the next person but allowing strangers to fight for my own amusement felt weird.

"Buttons," she mouthed back.

20

I looked down at my blouse as if I'd find a missing button or two before remembering my shirt didn't have buttons. I shook my head and gripped the knob tighter. "What?" I repeated.

She pointed at the door and mimicked, tossing a drink and circling her chest. "Buttons," she said meaningfully.

"Ah." But she'd left the restaurant earlier. "Are you sure?" I whispered.

Tippi nodded. "I'd prefer not to get into another fight tonight." Her voice was hushed and barely audible as she fidgeted with the bottom of her t-shirt.

I took my hand off the doorknob and reached back to take Tippi's hand. "Understood."

The argument grew louder.

"You need to go before Rhonda calls the cops again," a man said. I assumed it was Blake, but I couldn't be sure.

"I'm not afraid of Chief Dumbass or his minions. I know things—"

"Just stop it," the guy rasped as he cut her off. "Rhonda has control of this place."

"For now," the woman told him. There was a slight pause. "You and I both know that bitch faked the will. There's no way Uncle Tommy would have cut us out of the business."

"Shhh. Keep it down. She can't know what we're doing."

21

"I don't give a rat's fart what she knows. I want her so scared she'll piss herself stupid."

"Or she'll scramble to cross every T and dot every I. Don't be stupid, Darlene."

I leaned my ear against the door as his tone turned quietly seething.

"Don't blow this for us."

"Ow," she snapped. "You're hurting me."

I couldn't stand by and do nothing. I gestured for Tippi to step back and stay put as I rattled the door handle to warn the couple in the hall, waited a few seconds, and then cracked it open to peek out.

The hallway was empty.

I turned back to Tippi and shrugged. "They're gone."

She blinked. "That was intense."

"No kidding. You hungry?"

"Starved." Tippi gave me a tight smile. "You go first."

"Coward," I teased.

She gave a soft laugh. "I'm just trying to save another shirt."

The band was warming up onstage as if they'd all just returned. Tippi and I hastily made the trek to our table, where Pippa and Gilly waited for us. There was a glass of red wine and iced water behind my plate and sparkling grape juice behind Tippi's.

"I ordered appetizers." Gilly handed the menu to the younger Davenport. "Are you okay?"

"Just right," Tippi answered. "I'm sorry for the drama. This is supposed to be all about you, and I will ensure it stays that way." She crossed her heart with her hand. "No more excitement. At least not the kind that requires calling the law."

Gilly grinned. "One day, we'll all laugh about it."

Pippa grimaced and shook her head. "But today is *not* that day."

THREE

Whitecaps on the river sparkled with color as the sky turned salmon-pink and coral.

"Gorgeous," Pippa said quietly as she sipped her iced tea.

"One of the prettiest sunsets I've ever seen," Gilly agreed.

We hadn't had any plans for the rest of the evening, so the four of us had changed into comfortable lounging wear, grabbed some drinks and snacks, and sat out on the balcony to take in the view from the bluff top. Tippi still wore the t-shirt from La Sous Terre, but she'd changed into sweatpants.

"Why are you still in that top?" Pippa asked her.

"It's soft," Tippi answered.

Her older sister gave her a bland look. "Whatever."

"Sooo..." Gilly rubbed her hands together. "What's on the agenda for tomorrow?"

She was attempting to change the temperature between the two sisters, so I enthusiastically dove right in. "We have a winery tour at eleven a.m., so we'll need to get to the Blue Rooster Diner by nine-thirty-ish for breakfast." Blue Rooster was a local restaurant that served breakfast all day like a Bob Evans or a Denny's. The pictures and reviews online were stellar. "The winery and vineyard tours are an hour and end with lunch and a wine tasting at Corked, a bistro overlooking the river."

"That sounds...athletic," Gilly said diplomatically.

I laughed. "According to the website, it's a leisurely walk, but this is for you, so we can change the itinerary if you want."

She managed to look chagrinned. "No, it sounds lovely."

"As long as the weather holds," Pippa added.

My BFF's brow knitted with concern. "According to the weather app, there's a ten percent chance of rain."

I resisted rolling my eyes. "There is a ninety percent chance of sunshine and mildly warm temperatures."

Gilly didn't look convinced.

"I've packed some emergency ponchos, just in case," Pippa admitted. "One for each of us, just in case."

Gilly's shoulders relaxed. "Perfect."

I chuckled. "Such a mom."

Pippa gave me a light reprimand with the back of her fingers.

I leaned away and cried, "Child abuse."

Gilly giggled.

Tippi got up.

"Where are you going?" her sister asked.

She shook out her hands and then gestured toward the door. "Out for a jog to work off some energy."

"Don't go too close to the cliff ledge," Gilly warned. "Nothing ruins a girls' getaway like falling to your death."

I snorted iced tea out my nose and smacked Gilly on her thigh.

She winced. "Ow."

"I'll be back soon," Tippi said noncommittally. Her tone was distracted. I worried Pippa's fears might not be as far off base as I hoped.

"Have fun," I told her. She didn't need to know that I was also worried about her. "Take a flashlight in case it gets dark while you're out."

"Okay, Mom," she quipped.

"Hah," I countered. "Cool Aunt, maybe, but Mom? Never."

I'd never had the maternal urges of my friends. My desire to remain childless had cost me my first marriage. Luckily, my partner Ezra wasn't interested in children, at least not more children. He and his first wife had a son together. They'd both been sixteen at the time. His life had turned into full-time responsibility from that moment forward, and now that his son Mason was out of high school and off to college, Ezra had no interest in starting another family from scratch.

Still, it amazed me how some people judged our relationship from an outside lens, as if their points of view had anything to do with us. I'd heard whispers about how someone his age could never love a woman my age. Some jerk had even said it was biologically impossible for us to be together. Ezra and I had a good laugh about that as we biologied all over his cabin.

He loved me, and I loved him. No one else's opinion mattered. Opinions were like buttholes. Everyone had one, but I didn't want to see or hear them.

Pippa sighed heavily as the front door closed behind her sister. I rested my hand on her shoulder. "Try not to get in your head about it."

"Easier said than done."

My phone, charging on the kitchen counter, rang. Pippa half-smiled when I squeezed her shoulder before getting up. My heart fluttered when I saw Ezra's name on the screen. "Hello, handsome," I greeted him. "You just getting off work?"

His voice was low and soft as he answered. "Just walked in the door."

"You sound tired. Anything exciting happening in Garden Cove?"

"The usual," he said. "How about you? Miss me?"

"Terribly." I smiled. "And I'm fine. We had a little excitement here."

His tone perked up. "Oh yeah? Tell me about it."

"Tippi got in a fight with a local at dinner tonight."

Gilly championed Tippi. "In her defense, that local was spoiling for it."

"And Tippi didn't so much fight as stand there looking indignant," Pippa added.

"What happened?" Ezra asked.

"She was flirting with a man who happened to have a girlfriend. The girlfriend got stupid about it and threw a drink at her."

"The police were called," Gilly called out.

"The police?" Ezra sounded less excited and more concerned.

"It wasn't a big deal. They took Tippi's statement and our names, but the woman who'd started the fight had already left by then."

He chuckled. "So much for a few quiet days in wine country."

"It can still happen." I moved from the kitchen to my bedroom. "I do miss you," I told him. "When are you and Jordan doing your thing with Scott?"

"Tomorrow," Ezra said. "He's celebrating with some of his hospital friends and his younger brother tonight. We're going to do something more low-key tomorrow."

"Nice." I sat in the easy chair near the bedroom window and gazed at the trees peppering the yard. My room didn't have a bluff or river view, but it was still pretty. "We'll have to come back here sometime, just the two of us."

"It's a date," Ezra said. "Are you in for the night?"

"Yep. We were sipping iced tea out on the balcony watching the sunset."

"I'll let you get back to it." He paused for a moment, then said, "I like hearing your voice when the day is over."

My lips tugged up into a smile. "I like hearing *your* voice."

———

BREAKFAST HAD GONE off without a hitch. It had rained hard for about twenty minutes before it let up, and the sky turned blue again while we were eating. The sound of the shower bouncing on the roof of the diner had been oddly soothing. I'd had the best pecan pancakes with butter and maple syrup. Tippi and Pippa had eaten the Blue Rooster basic—two eggs, crispy hashbrowns, bacon, and toast. Gilly had gone for the sausage gravy and biscuits with a side of hashbrowns. By the time we'd made it to the winery for the tour, all of us were ready for naps.

There was a collective sigh in the car when I cut the engine and it was time to get out. Gilly rubbed her belly. "Maybe we shouldn't have carb loaded."

Tippi giggled. "Good thing Nora arranged a hike later."

"I'm thinking a nap," Pippa said. "Then we can think about a hike."

"Don't be a party pooper," Tippi told her sister.

"It's my lot in life," Pippa lamented. "You bring the party, and I'll bring the poop." Her stomach burbled, and she rubbed it.

I arched a brow at her.

"I'm fine," she said. "No one tells you that having a baby starts the downfall of your internal workings."

Gilly raised a hand. "I told you."

"Yeah, but you had twins. I thought it would be different for me."

I smirked. "Do we need to go back to the house before we do the winery tour?"

Pippa pressed her palm into her stomach and paused as if waiting for it to speak. When it didn't, she said, "No, we're good."

"I'm glad you and your stomach are on board." I looked at her, then Gilly. "Are we ready? The tour starts in five minutes, and they said we needed to be here ten minutes early."

"Whoa," Tippi exclaimed, then ducked down in her seat. "Crazy at ten o'clock."

I looked to the left and saw the back of a blonde woman in a blue shirt and jeans marching around the side of the building. I couldn't tell if it was the drink thrower from the night before, but it could've been. It didn't matter. She was gone now.

"I'm sure it will be fine," I said with a distinct lack of conviction. I hoped wherever the woman was heading it was far, far away from the tour.

I waited a few seconds for her to disappear before

ordering, "Everyone out." I shooed them. "It's too late to get a refund, so let's do it."

Tippi held out her hand when we got out of the car. "Keys," she said. "I am taking my DD job seriously."

I shrugged and handed them over. "Great, because I plan to try every wine available, and I don't plan to spit any of it out."

"I guess we won't be making the hike then," Gilly snarked. "What with you passing out before we get started."

I feigned incredulity. "I'm no lightweight."

"Sure, and the Pope isn't Catholic." Gilly had known me since the first day of kindergarten, and we'd done plenty of drinking and partying during high school, and it never took much to get me tipsy.

Even so, I was determined to show her a good time. "Fine. I'll spit."

"That's what she said," Gilly added with a laugh.

Tippi and Pippa chuckled as we followed a sign that pointed to the winery tasting room. Chief Terry, the police chief we'd met the night before, almost bowled me over as he pushed open the door on his way out.

"Pardon me, ladies," he apologized without looking up. His face was flushed, and he looked like a man on a mission. Was his visit business or pleasure? Maybe both. Either way, it wasn't my problem. This adventure was about Gilly, and I wouldn't let my curiosity spoil our fun.

"He didn't even recognize us," Tippi pointed out.

"I think he has other things on his mind." The light

tinkling of wind chimes sounded as I ushered my friends inside. The spacious storefront was painted buttercream with dark wood accents. Sweet fruits, spices, and aged oak hung in the air like perfume. I focused on holding off the memories the room held. The way they flipped through my mind, there were many.

There were scratches and chips on the edge of the hardwood bar and dust noticeably on the necks of the bottles lined up on a display shelf. Rhonda walked out of a door from the back, a forced smile on her lips as she gave the four of us a cursory once-over. Her button-down shirt was untucked on one side, and her hair was haphazardly loose around her reddened face. She looked like a woman who had just finished a fight.

The police chief had looked similarly disheveled, and I amended my thought.

Gilly raised her brow at me in a knowing look. She'd come to the same conclusion that I had. Rhonda and Chief Terry were hooking up. I wrinkled my nose, remembering the vision from the night before. Had it been Terry and Rhonda in the storeroom? Possibly. Had they been sleeping together since before her husband's death? Probably. Was it my business? Nope.

"Sorry I wasn't out here," Rhonda said. "You ladies are a little early."

"We were told to arrive ten minutes before the tour, but we can browse the shop for a bit if you're not ready," Pippa told her.

I knew my girl and her marketing brain. She wanted

to scope out the displays and labels. With our influx of online business, she'd hired a graphic designer to create a new logo to solidify our brand.

Rhonda rolled her shoulders back and plastered on a smile. "No, it's fine. We might as well get started."

"Great," Gilly said. "I'm looking forward to seeing how the sausage is made."

"Is this your first time to a winery?" Rhonda asked her.

"Not my first," Gilly admitted. "My hus—" She shook her head. "I trained as a sommelier one summer and did several vineyard tours in Italy. I found that every winery had its own vibe." Gilly's ex, Gio Rossi, was a top chef. Early in their marriage, when they'd been happily in love, Gilly had learned all about wine so that she could work with him in his restaurant. They spent a wonderful summer in Italy. The memory of that brief happiness had kept Gilly in the marriage long past its expiration date.

"Italy?" the woman looked mildly impressed. "We're no Barone Ricasoli, but we're one of the top vineyards in the Midwest."

I glanced at Gilly in askance.

"The oldest vineyard in Italy," she supplied. "It was established in the eleven-hundreds." Her expression grew wistful. "The place is amazing." She pivoted her gaze to Rhonda. "Have you been?"

"No, Tommy always said we would go, but we never quite made it."

"To Italy?" Gilly asked.

"To anywhere," Rhonda replied, her eyes distant. Suddenly, she snapped her attention to us. "If you ladies give me a minute, I'll grab Paul, and he can start your tour."

"Sounds great," I told her.

After Rhonda exited through the door behind the bar, Pippa made a face and said, "It's not just me, right? That was weird."

"It's not just you," Tippi granted. "She looked like she'd been in a tussle."

I snickered. "Tussle? Okay, Grandma."

Tippi blushed, then shook her head. "I've been hanging out with Maggie Elmore too much."

"Maggie?" Margaret Elmore was in her early eighties but still had the energy of a sixty-year-old. She used to run the fresh market in Garden Cove but retired years ago. "How do you know her?"

"She's my new..." Tippi shook her head, and her lips quirked up in an embarrassed smile. "Damn it. It's anonymous for a reason."

"Ah." I inclined my head. "She's a good one."

"Yeah." Tippi picked at a stray hair that clung to the sleeve of her shirt. "She is."

FOUR

A man strode through the door Rhonda had exited. "You must be the Gilly Party." I recognized him as one of the band members from the night before. If memory served me correctly, he was the drink thrower's brother. "I'm Paul Nichols, enologist for Rivière Tranquille. Welcome." He smiled amiably, looking through us like we weren't there.

I recognized the expression. I'd probably had it myself during long, busy summer weeks at the shop. There was only so much jubilant interaction I could take before I started to go mind-numb. However, we looked to be the day's first customers, and I wanted this experience to be memorable for Gilly.

I put my smile on high beam. "Hey there. We sure are." I waited for a second until his eyes met mine. "My best friend," I gestured to Gilly, "is getting married this weekend, and this is her party."

He seemed to startle at my intense eye contact. I couldn't blame him, I probably looked deranged, but by golly, my BFF would be getting this guy's full attention if I had to stare it out of him.

"We're excited," Gilly added, diffusing the manic energy.

Paul nodded, but the tension at the corner of his eyes didn't ease as he made eye contact with all of us. The corner of his lip tugged into a half-smile as a hint of recognition filled his expression. "You all were at La Sous Terre last night."

Tippi stealthily ducked behind her sister.

"Yep," I said. "But we're here today." I'll admit my tone was slightly blunt, but I didn't want the drama of the night before marring our visit.

"Fair enough." Paul's half-smile turned into a grin. "Let me get everyone started with a taste of our 2019 Chardonel while I tell you about our history." He was tall and thin with hazel eyes. Not unattractive, but not as obviously handsome as Blake, the lead singer. On his own, though, I could see him turning a couple of heads.

He pulled a chilled bottle of wine from below the bar. "This particular vintage was crafted from late-ripened white grapes. His grin turned devilish as he turned the label to us. "We call it Wise Old Broad."

"Hah," I scoffed. "Okay, then." Internally, I thought, *well-played*.

He took out four small, clear plastic tasting cups.

"Only three." Pippa put a hand over the fourth cup.

Tippi's lips pursed into a tight pout briefly as she gave her sister an incredulous glance. Before Pippa could take note, she made her expression bland. Poor girl. She'd been sober for a couple of years now, and she'd done an incredible job of caring for my goddaughter J.J. Had something changed to make Pippa obsess about the idea that her sister was backsliding? I knew enough from my talks with Jordy, Pippa's husband, that an addict was always an addict, even when sober, and the same was true of an alcoholic.

"None for me," Tippi told him. "But I'll take sparkling water if you have it."

"Our designated driver," I added, trying to take the sting out of Pippa's course correction.

Paul nodded and gave the younger Davenport sister a sympathetic smile. "A DD is always a good idea."

Tippi's smile was genuine now. "Somebody has to keep the Wise Old Broads out of trouble."

Gilly snorted a laugh, and I said in mock hurt, "Hey, watch it."

Tippi giggled. Pippa still looked ill at ease. If she kept bringing down the mood, she would find herself confined to the cabin for the rest of our trip.

I leaned my shoulder into hers and whispered, "No party likes a pooper."

"Sorry," she whispered back.

I gave her a quick wink, then turned back to our tour

guide. "Let's see if the Wise Old Broad is as tasty and attractive as her name."

Paul chuckled. "It's one of my favorites." He uncorked the bottle, gave it a slight swirl then poured a small amount into each tasting cup.

"Does it need to be decanted?" Pippa asked.

Gilly answered, "White wines don't need to be decanted, usually, and if they have a lot of aromatics in them, a decanting can lessen the experience."

Paul arched a brow at her. "Exactly right."

Tippi took the sparkling water he offered her and asked, "What's an enologist?"

"It's a fancy name for a winemaker," a woman said as she entered the room from a side door. It was the waitress Donna from the restaurant.

"It's a little more than that," Paul defended. "An enologist is a wine scientist. I have a double degree in viticulture and food fermentation." I could hear the pride in his voice.

"And still, Tommy left the vineyard to my mom." Donna shook her head. Then, as if she realized she had an audience, she rolled her shoulders back, and her demeanor took on a more relaxed visage. Her gaze met mine, and she shrugged. "Family stuff. Sorry. Paul really is one of the best vintners in the Midwest. Enjoy your tour." On that pleasantry, she strolled behind the bar and exited the way of Rhonda.

Paul's jaw clenched as he turned his attention back to us. "If you ladies want to taste the wine, I'll describe what you should be tasting as you tease it over your tongue."

"Can I give it a go?" Gilly requested enthusiastically. "I'd like to test my palate."

"Absolutely," Paul replied.

I picked up my cup and gave the wine a sip, swallowing the slightly acidic but not unpleasant dry wine while Gilly swished it around in her mouth and played with hers.

"I taste pears..."

Paul nodded.

Gilly continued, "Maple...and..." She gave the vintner a quizzical look. "Is that pecan?"

His smile widened in pleasure. "Yes. Most people guess vanilla and hazelnut. You have an excellent palate."

Gilly blushed at the compliment. "It's delicious."

"Just like breakfast," Tippi said as she sipped her sparkling water. When Paul looked at her, she added, "Maple and pecans. Sounds like it would pair well with pancakes." She giggled.

Paul shook his head but laughed. "Pancakes are one of the many foods it would pair well with." He glanced at the rest of us. "If you're ready, we'll start the tour."

"Lead on, MacDuff," Gilly quipped.

"Who is MacDuff, and why do we need him to lead?" Tippi mused to me as we followed Paul through the side door of the tasting room.

She must have skipped English literature when she

was in private school. "He was the avenging character in Macbeth." MacBeth murdered MacDuff's wife and children. MacDuff, in revenge, raised an army to go to war against MacBeth. The original phrase, "Lay on, MacDuff," was said by MacBeth as he ordered his army to attack MacDuff. Over the years, the phrase had turned into "lead on, Macduff," meaning for someone to take the lead. A much more pleasant and less violent resolve. Just the way I liked it.

Paul led us on a short walk to the winemaking building behind the shop. "Rivière Tranquille Vineyard was established by my great-great-grandfather Lieutenant Rigel Nichols in 1934," Paul said as he led us past large metal vats. "This is where the grapes are crushed and pressed. Harvest happens from August through October, so we don't have any grapes going through this process." He explained how the liquid and solids are separated, the fermentation process, and how they age the wine in oak barrels from three months to three years.

There were four pictures of gentlemen hanging on the wall. The fourth picture was Paul, wearing a dark suit with a gold lapel pin bearing the letters AZ.

I didn't need to ask because Paul said, "These are the four vintners that have created every bottle of wine for Rivière Tranquille since we pressed our first grapes. The first is Rigel, our founder, and Jonathan, his oldest son, Thomas, my uncle, and finally me."

Gilly peered closer at Paul's picture. "Hey, you are an Alpha Zeta."

"I am," he said brightly. "I was invited to join during my sophomore year at college."

"Fancy," Tippi muttered.

Gilly said, "It's an honor. From what I hear, they only invite the most promising students into their group. One of my mentors in Italy belonged to the Alpha Zeta branch in Napa Valley."

Paul beamed with pride as his fingers absently touched his lapel. Then he frowned. "We better get back on track, or we'll be late for the wine tasting."

"We wouldn't want that!" Gilly smiled at him. She was enjoying herself, and that made me happy.

"Okay." I bounced up on the balls of my feet. "What's next, Mr. Winemaker?"

He opened the door to the fermentation room, and a sweetly pungent, woodsy scent filled the space.

"What are you doing?" a man says. He knocks a white baggie of powder out of a taller, thinner man's hands. "Keep that crap out of my wine."

"Adding sulfites keeps the wine from spoiling." I recognize the voice of the lanky man as our tour guide, Paul. "We had to throw out fifty barrels of wine this spring that had turned into pure vinegar."

"The way we make wine is the way my father made it and his father made it. If you don't like it, you can start your own winery. Traditions matter, boy."

His father and his father's father. This had to be Tom Nichols, Rhonda's dead husband.

"People rode horses before cars were invented, Uncle

Tommy. It doesn't make riding horses a better means of transportation."

That confirmed that it was indeed the deceased owner.

Tommy made a loud "Bah!" sound as he waved his hand. "Get rid of that crap, and don't let me catch you trying to use it again, or I'll take you out like the trash you're trying to turn my wine into."

As Tommy walked away, Paul muttered, "Someone needs to take you out, old man."

By the time the vision ended, we were leaving out the back door, and I'd missed the rest of the winemaking part of the tour.

I raised my hand. "Do you add sulfites to your wine?"

"To the pressed grapes before we add the sugar," Paul answered. "It prevents spoiling during the fermentation process."

I arched my brow. So much for tradition. I wondered if he'd waited until after his uncle's funeral to start using the additive.

"Does it change the taste of the wine?"

"Not really," Paul said. "Sulfites are a natural byproduct of the fermentation process, but sometimes it can go awry, and the wine can go bad. Adding it stops that from happening."

I nodded.

"That's so interesting," Tippi said. "I had no idea so much went into making a bottle of wine." She smiled, her eyelashes fluttering in Paul's direction.

I smiled and shook my head. The girl was going to flirt her way through the vineyard, and more power to her. She couldn't drink, so she had to find her fun in other ways.

"During World War I, the French Resistance gave British soldiers shelter in cavernous wine cellars throughout France," Paul continued as he guided us to a six-seater golf cart. "Rigel developed a friendship with the owner of the Chateau de Tranquille vineyard. After the war, he returned to the vineyard and fell in love with winemaking. Before moving to America, he married Annalise Renault, the vintner's daughter, and as a wedding present, he was gifted with forty French-American hybrid grape starters. Rigel moved his wife and newborn son to Missouri in 1931 and bought an existing vineyard and the surrounding land." He gestured to the cart. "If you ladies hop on, I'll take you to one of our fields that are just starting to fruit."

"Nineteen Thirty-One?" I asked. "That was during prohibition."

Paul nodded. "The prior vineyard operation had gone out of business because of the illegality of alcohol production. My great-grandfather took a chance on the business in hopes that prohibition wouldn't last." He turned the key, and the golf cart started with a slight jerk. "Two years later, prohibition ended, and the year after that, our grapevines were trained and bearing fruit for the first Rivière Tranquille. A red Chambourcin wine that he named for his wife, Annalise."

"Aww, that's so sweet," Gilly said. "He must've loved her very much."

Paul drove us down a dirt road along rows of grapevines. "I think he did. She died the year of their first harvest. My great-grandfather remarried my grandmother, Bella, but he never forgot his Annalise."

"That's so sad," Pippa said. "She moved all the way to America, leaving her family behind, only to die after a few years."

As we came to a stop, Paul pointed toward a familiar white stone and stucco building.

"Hey, that's La Sous Terre," I said. This must've been our view the evening before.

"Yep," he confirmed. "The restaurant has been a huge part of making our vineyards a destination hot spot, with classic French cuisine with a Midwest twist."

"I can't attest that the food was delicious," Pippa interjected.

"Our vineyards are all trained and ready to start bearing fruit this year. Most of the wine that is made in this state is German," Paul went on. "But as I said earlier, our vines are French-American hybrids, which makes them unusual for Missouri. We have Chardonel grapes, which make a crisp and acidic wine; Vignoles, which make a sweeter, honied-tasting wine; and Traminette for making dryer, more floral wines."

"What kind of grapes are German grapes?" I asked, genuinely curious. Unlike Gilly, I was a casual wine drinker, and I hadn't realized there were so many different types of grapes.

"Riesling," Paul answered, "But German wineries in Missouri also use a lot of American grapes like the Norton, Concord, and Catawba. The German wines tend to be fruitier and sweeter than French wines."

"Mmmm," I mused. "Sounds like dessert."

Paul pulled the golf cart over. "We'll get out here and walk through the vineyard to Corked, our bistro overlooking the river, for lunch and a proper varietal tasting of the wines we sell in our store."

"Sounds great," Gilly said enthusiastically.

I was still full from breakfast, but I wasn't about to spoil her good mood. Besides, it was a beautiful day out, and I had on my walking shoes. Paul's last name was Nichols, and I was curious as to how he fit into the family.

"Was your father Tom Nichols' brother?"

Paul gave me a sharp look, then said, "Yes. Older brother." His tone held some ire. "My dad died in 1990. He was only thirty-two."

"How old were you?" Tippi asked, her voice full of compassion.

"I was three." Paul gestured to some small green clusters of grapes on a vine. "Here are the Vignoles. These ripen faster than the Chardonel and will be ready for harvest sometime in late August, early September. As you can see by the many clusters already starting, these vines are fully trained, and we'll be able to produce about fifty thousand gallons of Pinot in the fall."

"Wowza," Pippa said. "That's a whole lot of grapes."

Paul chuckled. "It sure is."

We followed him down the long row as he explained the fertilization and watering needed to keep the crops healthy. A great shadow passed over us as a dark cloud hid the sun. I peered up. "Where did that come from?"

"Are they calling for rain?" Gilly asked as she took out her phone and woke up the screen. The proverbial "they" was the weather app on her smartphone. She slowed her pace to study the radar. The rest of us kept pace with Paul.

"Come on, slowpoke," I told her.

"I'm coming." She waved me on. "I'll catch up."

"It's Missouri." Paul cast a glance at me and shrugged. "The weather changes every few minutes."

"You're so right." Tippi twirled a lock of her blonde hair around her finger. "I've only lived here a few years, and I can't believe how it can be a hundred degrees one day and then snowing the next."

"Is your grandfather still alive?" I probed. I knew his uncle was deceased, but Thomas might have taken over before his father died.

The skin between Paul's eyes pinched. Clearly, he didn't love personal questions, but he answered me anyhow. "Rigel died in 1981, and my grandfather, Jonathan, died in 2002. That's when Uncle Tommy inherited the vineyard."

"Thank you," I told him. "I'm not trying to pry. My mother died a few years ago, and I still find it hard to talk about."

"Oh, look." Paul pointed ahead at an A-Frame building at the end of the row. "That's Corked. There's a beautiful view of the river from the terrace."

I had to give it to him. It had been a smooth change of topic. I glanced back at Gilly, and she was holding up her phone and turning in a half circle. I let out a bark of warning as her left foot backed into the vines, and her shoe got ensnared by the snaking plants. An expletive that I won't repeat flew from her mouth as she smacked the ground with the front of her body.

"Gilly!" I shouted and ran back to her.

"I'm fine," she called back with a lot of indignation. "The only thing hurt is my pride and maybe my elbow." She slowly rolled to her side, and Paul was right behind me when I reached to help her from the ground.

"I can get up myself," Gilly complained. She put her hand down, her fingers brushing some kind of mesh covering the ground at the base of the vines, then let out a surprised shriek as she yanked her hand away and scrambled to her feet.

"What's wrong?" Pippa asked.

"There's something under those leaves," Gilly said. "It was cold and..." She rubbed her arms as if to ward off the cold. "Like a dead, hairless rodent or something."

I reached down as Paul said, "Don't—"

Too late. I lifted the lush vine, full of large green leaves. "Oh, no." I touched my mouth with my free hand.

"What is it?" Tippi asked.

The cold dead thing hadn't been a rodent. "It's a hand," I said numbly. And sitting on the ring finger was an emerald-cut diamond with a halo of smaller diamonds around the stone and along the band. I gave Paul a sympathetic look. "I think it's your sister."

Heaven knows I wanted to be wrong, but as that diamond glistened in the afternoon sun on the lifeless pale hand under the mesh, I knew I wasn't.

"My sister? Darlene?" Paul's hands dropped to his side. "What are you talking about?" He blinked rapidly as he took Gilly by the arm and started tugging her away. "We should get on with the tour."

"Paul," I said sharply as I lifted the mesh. "Maybe this isn't your sister, but it's definitely a person." I turned my attention to Pippa. "Call nine-one-one."

She blanched as she retrieved her phone from her pocket and turned her back on the scene.

Paul let go of Gilly and stalked over to where we found the hand. "This isn't..."

As he reached down, I tried to stop him. "Don't touch anything. We need to wait for the police."

The young man didn't listen. Instead, he yanked the

mesh up, exposing more of the body. "Darlene," Paul choked. He staggered back. Gilly mommed-up and put a comforting hand on his back.

Now that some of the body was exposed, I knelt for a closer look. Darlene's face was ashen gray and covered with smudges of makeup and dirt. Her left upper arm had circular bruises, and there were scratches above her wrist. Her index fingernail was partially torn and hanging from the cuticle. She wore the same red shirt she'd had on the night before. Or at least one that was similar.

"How?" Paul asked.

"Maybe it was an accident," Tippi said. "She was pretty drunk last night."

Paul glared at her. "My sister could be impulsive, but she wasn't a drunk."

Tippi raised her hand. "No offense meant."

Pippa had walked off toward the winery, trying to get good reception.

"This wasn't an accident," I said. After all, the mesh hadn't crawled itself over her body. Someone tried to hide Darlene, and the fact that they hadn't moved the body somewhere less conspicuous told me that the someone who covered her up had been short on time.

I leaned close to see if I could smell anything unusual.

"What are you doing?" Paul's tone was accusing.

I reached over and touched Darlene's wrist. Her skin was cold and hard. She'd been here for a while, which meant she hadn't been the woman we'd seen walking behind the store. "Checking to make sure she doesn't have a pulse." That she was dead was obvious, but families and loved ones needed confirmation.

"And?" he asked, a hint of hope in the question.

I shook my head. "She's dead."

He threw his hands up with a sob. "She did this," he accused. "This is her fault!" I wasn't sure if the "she" he was talking about was Darlene or someone else, but it sounded like he'd developed a theory in his head as to how his sister had ended up as part of the tour.

Paul started toward the body, then abruptly turned on his heel and paced twenty feet away.

Pippa trotted back to us, her face flushed. "The police are on their way."

I stood up and dusted my hands. "I guess all we can do now is wait."

"No, no, no." Gilly pulled me aside and whispered, "This is truly awful, but I'm getting married in three days. Promise me you won't stick your *nose* into this mess."

"I promise," I told her. I had no intention of investigating. I didn't know the police in Marseille, and they didn't know me. Chances were good they wouldn't believe me if I told them about my gift, and if I knew too much about the crime, they would probably assume I had something to do with it. Nope. Gilly had nothing to worry about. Nora Black, Psychic Detective, was closed for business on this one. We'd give our witness statements, then go along our merry way. "I'm keeping my *nose* out of it."

"Good. I don't want to sound like a bridezilla. I feel terrible for that poor girl."

I gave my friend a sympathetic look. "I get it. This wasn't the fun trip I had planned for you. Once we're done here, we'll go back to the cabin, pack up, and get the hell out of Dodge."

Gilly's shoulder's slumped, and the pinched lines around her eyes softened. "Thank you."

"No worries," I told her. "I got you."

Pippa and Tippi joined us. "We're going back to Garden Cove this afternoon," I told them. "We'll give our statements and be done."

Pippa looked as relieved as Gilly. "Good."

Tippi nodded. "I don't want to be here any longer than necessary.

"What did you tell the police?" I asked Pippa.

"I told them where we were and that we found a body in the vineyard on the path to Corked." She sucked her teeth. "What an awful mess."

I sighed. "That seems to be the consensus."

Gilly twirled her engagement ring with her thumb. "Did they give you any instructions?"

"Nope," Pippa said. "They just said to stay put, and someone would be out to investigate."

Tippi cringed. "So, we have to stay here with the body?"

"You go on down to Corked," I told her. "All of you. I'll stay here with Paul and wait for the police to arrive."

Gilly shook her head. "I'm not leaving you behind."

"Don't think of it as leaving me behind." I pointed to the two people coming from the A-frame. "Think of it as stopping the flow of traffic."

"And how am I supposed to do that?"

"You're a people person. Go people."

She shook her head. "Fine. But you holler if anything happens."

"Unless zombies are real, I think I can handle it."

Gilly rolled her eyes, but I could tell she was freaked out. Honestly, she wasn't the only one. I'd stumbled over a dead body before, but it didn't mean I was immune to the horror of it. This poor girl had been cut down in the prime of her life. There was nothing routine about her death.

I walked over to Paul. "I'm so sorry for your loss," I sympathized. "Is there anyone you want to call?"

"No." He stared toward the main road. I could hear sirens in the distance.

"What about her fiancé?"

"Her fianc— Oh. Blake." His eyes narrowed, and his lips thinned. "He should've been with her. This is his fault."

First, it had been "her" fault and now "his." Paul was liberal with his blame. I understood, though. The anger that came with grief needed a bad guy, someone to be at fault. It was the brain's way of trying to make the death of a loved one make sense. In this case, though, someone *was* to blame. There was literally a bad guy.

I had promised Gilly I wouldn't investigate, and I meant it. However, I couldn't stop myself from asking the question, "Why do you think it's his fault?"

"Blake is a cheating asshole. He and Darlene have been together off and on since high school, and their breakups are always about one thing. He can't keep his hands off other women." He narrowed his gaze at me. "You don't think I remember you all from last night? What do you think that jerk was doing with your friend at the bar?"

"So, you think he killed your sister because she was going to break up with him again?"

His eyes widened. "No. I don't think Blake..." His words trailed off. "I'm going to be sick." And on that declaration, he pivoted and threw up on the nearest vine.

Gilly, Pippa, and Tippi were talking with the older couple who'd been on the path, keeping them from getting closer, and two men in uniform were hustling toward us from the winery with Rhonda Nichols close behind.

"The police are here," I told Paul. I was ready for the authorities to take over. "Again, I'm so very sorry."

He wiped his mouth with the back of his hand, and his gaze followed mine. His lip curled up in a snarl. "Bitch," he muttered.

Since Rhonda was the only female in the bunch, I

assumed his pique was directed at her. "You really don't like your aunt."

"Arrest her," he shouted to the cops as he shoved past me.

I recognized one of the officers as the young man with Chief Terry the night before. He stepped in front of Paul before he could reach Rhonda.

"Calm down, now," the officer ordered. "Tell me the situation."

Paul tried to take a swing at the officer. Total mistake. He was on the ground, arm behind his back, and howling in pain.

"I told you to calm down." The officer looked at me. "Why don't you fill me in?"

I gestured to the arm and head uncovered at the base of the grapevines. "We found her when we were taking the tour. Around ten to fifteen minutes ago. I lifted the mesh off her to get a better look and felt for a pulse, but otherwise, we haven't disturbed any part of the scene."

Rhonda gasped. "Is that Darlene?"

"Like you don't know," Paul grunted out. "Get off me, Copper," he told the officer. "Let me up!"

I thought calling the officer holding him down "copper" was oddly archaic, but maybe Paul was a fan of old mob movies.

"You going to behave?"

"Yes."

"Good." The officer got off Paul and helped him up. He jerked his hand back and gestured for his partner.

"Travis, go back to the car. Call Chief Porter and the coroner and let them know we have a body." Chief Terry had to be Chief Porter. Rhonda had called him Terry, and that's what had stuck in my mind, but most likely, his name was Terry Porter. Copper continued his instructions. "It's probable foul play, so bring back some crime scene tape and some stakes, so we can secure the scene." He waved at Paul, Rhonda, and me. "I'm going to need you three to go wait over at Corked until we're finished. We'll get your accounts of what happened after."

A rumble in the distance sounded. "Officer..." I said.

"Copper," he replied.

I shuffled uncomfortably at the joke. "Uhm, what's your name?"

"Connor Copper, ma'am."

"Oh." I had to readjust my thinking. "Officer Copper, you might want to get a tarp put up quickly." I turned my gaze to the sky. More dark clouds had joined the first one. "There's no telling what evidence the rain will wash away."

He looked startled for a moment, then nodded. "Good thinking." Travis was already on his way to the cruiser, and Copper appeared perplexed as droplets spattered against the dusty path.

Rhonda's eyes were red and rimmed with tears. I had gotten the feeling Darlene and her hadn't been close. After all, she'd called the police on her at the restaurant. However, the woman looked genuinely upset.

I caught her attention and asked, "You must have canopies that you all use for events."

She wrinkled her nose and sniffed. "We do."

"I'll get one," Paul said, and he took off in a sprint toward the winery.

Rhonda let out a heavy sigh. "I'll help him. He has no idea how I have sorted the sizes. How big of a canopy do you need?"

Copper seemed to calculate the area for a moment. "A twenty by twenty, if you have it."

"We do," Rhonda told him, then went jogging after Paul. I wasn't sure that letting those two be alone during the current situation was a good idea, but I held my tongue. I was a witness, not an investigator, and I would keep my opinions to myself. I only hoped the police didn't end up with two homicides to investigate.

Copper assessed me with a once-over. "That was quick thinking about the canopy. Do you work in law enforcement?"

I will not investigate. I will not investigate. "Nope. No law enforcement. I make lotions and soaps for a living."

"Huh." He frowned. "Either way, I appreciate a cool head."

"I'd say I was glad to be of service, but..." I tilted my head toward Darlene. "I would've preferred an uneventful day of good food and good wine. My best friend is getting married, and this wasn't on the agenda." I felt petty and small for a micro-moment. After all,

RENEE GEORGE

Darlene hadn't asked to die and have her body planted amongst the grapevines. "Did you know Darlene?"

"Darlene was a few years ahead of me in school. I didn't really know her, though. And Paul was off to college before I made it to high school. Still, you can't grow up in this town without knowing the Nichols. My older brother worked as a harvester for a couple of summers when he was in college."

"But not you?" I asked.

"Nah." He shrugged. "It's a lot of hours in the sun." There was a flash of lightning and a crash of thunder. I saw Gilly, Pippa, and Tippi rushing to the A-frame for shelter. The wind kicked up as the rain began in earnest. A tornado siren began to wail.

Another burst of lightning raised the hair on my arms. "We have to find a way to cover the body," I shouted over the roaring wind. I hugged my purse to me, then remembered the rain poncho Pippa had thrown in my purse the night before.

"Go!" Officer Copper ordered. "Get to Corked. It has a basement."

I shoved the poncho packet into his hand. "Here," I told him. "Use this to cover what you can."

The wind suddenly died down, and the rain stopped. Copper's eyes widened. "Go," he said again. "Run."

CHAPTER
SIX

My knees ached as we sat on the concrete floor of a small, cool wine cellar below Corked. Metal bottle racks lined one wall, and two large fridges were up against the far end of the damp room. The place held an earthy scent that reminded me of old paperback books. Slightly musty but not unpleasant. Other than the loud hum of the wine chillers, I couldn't hear the storm or the siren.

It was chilly enough that my knees ached a little. The older couple that had tried to leave earlier were huddled on the other side of the cellar, and a tearful, young blonde who I recognized from the night before was perched on the bottom stair. It was Ellie, the young woman who had escorted her drunk cousin from the restaurant. Her hair was similar in color to Darlene's and so was her build. On top of that, she wore a blue top and jeans. Since Darlene was cold and dead, it had to have been Ellie we'd seen marching away from the wine store. Looking at her now, I could see why Tippi had thought it was Darlene.

I leaned my shoulder into Gilly's. "I'm sorry. This is not the relaxing bachelorette vacay I'd had in mind for you when I booked this trip."

"It's not your fault." I detected a slight tone of accusation in her voice that I wrote off as stress. She was shaking her phone as if the movement would spontaneously give her four bars. "I can't believe it's pouring rain outside. The weather app said there was only a ten percent chance of storms today."

"We should take that weather app to Vegas," I teased.

Gilly's brown eyes focused on me and she groaned, "Too soon. After I'm safely married, you can joke all you want."

"Sorry." I couldn't help but think about all the trace evidence being washed away in the field. I wondered if Officer Copper had managed to get Darlene covered with the poncho before he sought shelter. Of course, better that evidence was lost than another life.

Pippa and Tippi were on the other side of me, both looking miserable.

Pippa said, "Do you really think there's a tornado out there?"

"If there was ever a time not to be sober," Tippi joked.

Pippa didn't laugh.

"What is going on?" her sister asked. "You've been acting weird for weeks."

"Nothing," Pippa muttered before shifting the conversation. "What do you think happened to that girl? Did you get any...?" She touched her nose.

I shook my head. "Nothing." I leaned forward to look around Pippa to Tippi. "She came back to the restaurant last night. Tippi and I overheard her outside the bathroom talking to a man."

"What man?" Gilly asked.

"I don't know. His voice was muffled, but he wasn't happy with her." I glanced over to Ellie. What happened after Darlene had left the restaurant the first time? Why had she come back to La Sous Terre after being ordered to leave?

"She said something about their uncle not cutting them out of the will," Tippi added.

"Do you think it was Paul?" Pippa asked. "I mean, the one talking to her in the hallway?"

"Maybe. But it seems like you can't spit around her without hitting a relative." I made a subtle gesture toward the crying cousin. "She might know. She'd been with Darlene earlier. Darlene might have confided in her."

"Nora..." Gilly's tone held a warning.

"Don't worry," I assured her. "I'm not investigating."

She didn't look reassured.

I couldn't blame her. My track record with ignoring murder wasn't good. But in this case, she could rest easy.

I wanted nothing more than to get the hell out of Falcon Crest and back home. Besides, I missed Ezra. I dug my phone from my purse. One bar.

Speaking of Ezra, I had a missed text from him.

Thinking of you. Hope you're having a good time. Can't wait to see you on Friday.

There was a second line of emojis that included a taco, an eggplant, and some fireworks. It made me smile.

A soft sob and a hard nose blow drew my attention. The blonde woman tucked a tissue into her pocket and hugged her knees to her chest.

I got up.

Gilly frowned. "What are you doing?" she asked suspiciously.

"I'm just going to go check on her," I said quietly. "No big deal." I wasn't investigating. I was being a good neighbor. At least, that's the excuse I was going with. I crossed the room to Ellie. "I'm sorry about your cousin."

"What?" she dabbed at her eyes. "How did you—"

"We were at La Sous Terre last night," I explained. "My friend over there is the one that your cousin threw a drink on."

"I'm so embarrassed," Ellie said. "I didn't even realize."

"And why would you? It was a brief encounter, and this awful thing that's happened trumps everything that came before it."

"I just don't understand how this happened. Your friend with dark hair told me it was Darlene, but I still can't believe it. Why was she in the vineyard in the first place?"

"You left with her last night. Did she say anything to you?"

Ellie shook her head. "She was so angry. She'd told me she wanted to call off her engagement, but she said that every time she got drunk."

"So, you didn't take it seriously?"

"No." The young blonde raised her hands. "She lives within walking distance of the restaurant. I dropped her by her house and went home."

"Did she mention her aunt Rhonda?"

Ellie scoffed. "She hated Rhonda. Tommy's first wife was like a mother to Paul and Darlene after their father died."

When I furrowed my brow, she explained, "Their mother ran away after the funeral, and no one has heard from her since. Tommy and Jen took them in and raised them like they were their own."

"What happened to Jen?"

"She passed away seven years ago of a heart condition. Two years later, Tommy married Rhonda."

"Wow." No wonder Darlene and her brother were angry that the vineyard and the business had been left to the wife. She'd only been the wife for a short time. "And how are you related?"

"My mom is Tommy's younger sister."

"She's still alive?"

"Yep." She frowned. "Momma is a bookkeeper for

the bank here in Marseille. She used to run the accounts for Rivière Tranquille, but after Tommy remarried..." She let the implication hang. From what I could surmise, everyone thought Rhonda was a gold-digging destroyer of families.

"How long ago did Tommy die?"

"Three months ago."

"Not that long ago." That meant the other members of the family were still in the contestation window, but they would have to make a case fast before the will was finalized.

Ellie sniffed. "And now, Darlene. It's just not right."

I squeezed Ellie's shoulder with sympathy. "Again, I am so sorry."

The cellar door opened with a clang, and I nearly jumped out of my skin.

"False alarm," Copper shouted down into the cellar. "Just a downburst on the other side of town."

Yikes.

The woman across the room said, "Oh, thank God," as the man with her stood up and then helped her get to her feet. "Let's get out of here, Milton, before something else happens."

"Agreed," said Gilly. My friends got up from the floor as well.

The woman slipped on a wet spot and grabbed the nearest wine rack for balance.

"Watch out," Ellie said sharply. "That one's loose."

The wire holding up one of the many bottles came

undone, and the wine slipped from its cradle and crashed to the floor. The spray of liquid hit my legs.

The woman and her husband danced away from the breakage. "Oh, my," she said. "I didn't mean to—"

"No worries," Ellie told her, a sigh heavy in her tone. "Accidents happen. Go on upstairs. There are napkins on the counter if you need to clean up."

I stooped down to help Ellie pick up some of the larger pieces of glass, and the sweet aroma of fermented grapes took me into a memory.

I hear heavy pants and moans over the constant humming of the fridges. The lights are off, so I can't see who's making the noises. There is movement, then a clatter as they hit the wine racks. A bottle makes a sharp pop as it hits the floor.

"Crap," a man whispers. His height and build make me think of Paul, but there's nothing that I can nail down to confirm it's him. "We need to get that damn rack fixed."

"Shhhh." The second voice sounds female, and there's a tinkle that sounds like delicate metal clicking together. They are talking so quietly that it's hard to tell. "Let's get out of here before someone comes downstairs."

"We should get it cleaned up," the man says. "We can't just leave the mess."

"You go ahead," the woman tells him. "I'll take care of it."

The cellar door opens, and light floods in. A woman stands in the doorway. She's a curvy blonde. I can't see her face, but I'm pretty sure it's Ellie until she opens her mouth.

"Well, isn't this cozy?" Her question is smug and self-satisfied, like the cat who ate the canary, and I recognize her voice. It's Darlene.

The memory faded. Ellie's stare was intense. "Are you okay? You were gone for a moment?"

"Fine," I told her. "Just had a little déjà vu."

Who had Darlene caught in the cellar? And when? And is that the reason she's dead? These were great questions, but questions that I didn't need to know the answers to.

Gilly called to me from the bottom stair. "You coming?"

"Yep. Be right there. "I handed the intact neck of the broken bottle to Ellie. "Sorry again," I told her. "Do you need anything?"

"Can you bring my best friend back?" I heard real grief in her voice. Darlene might have rubbed some people the wrong way, but Ellie genuinely cared. I didn't know what I'd do if anything happened to Gilly or Pippa. The two of them were my glue.

I gave her hand a light pat. "I really wish I could."

CHAPTER
SEVEN

Chief Terry Porter had on a gray rain suit over his clothing. Travis and Copper were putting up stakes in a perimeter around the area where we had discovered the body. Rhonda crossed her arms over her chest as she watched investigators destroy an eight-foot section of her grapevines. "Do you have to be so rough? Those plants are fifteen years old, and they aren't easily replaced."

"Shut up, Rhonda!" Paul squelched. "That's my sister under there. They can tear up the whole damn vineyard if that's what it takes."

"Since it's not your *damn* vineyard, it's not your *damn* choice," Rhonda countered.

Ellie hustled past me as she made her way to Paul. She put her arms around him and buried her face against his shoulder. His arms were limp against his sides, and he barely acknowledged his cousin.

Chief Porter's gaze met mine. He ran his fingers through his salt and pepper hair, then waved me to come over. As I approached him, I could see that Copper had used my poncho to cover what he could of Darlene. Good. I hope the rain hadn't ruined her chance for speedy justice.

"Chief," I greeted.

"Ms. Black," he said. "We have got to stop meeting like this."

"It's a habit I'd like to break." I rubbed my upper eyelid to keep it from twitching. "What an awful thing to have happened."

Chief Porter relaxed his stance. "Why don't you and your friends walk me through everything."

"Sure." My eye-twitching worsened. This was the last thing I'd imagined I'd be doing this week. Gilly was going to make me turn in my best friend card. "Do you want to talk to all of us at once or one at a time?"

"Is there a reason we need to separate you all? You're witnesses, not suspects." He arched a brow. "Or is there some reason I should think differently?"

"Nope." I cast a glance back at Pippa, Tippi, and Gilly, then back to the man in charge. "We're strictly tourists."

"Uhm-hmm." He gave me a quizzical stare. "Copper told me you had the scene locked down like someone with some law enforcement experience."

"That's kind of him to say."

"If I look you up, am I going to find anything interesting?"

"About boring old me?"

He narrowed his gaze at me. "I'm guessing there's not a whole lot about you that's boring, and you're not that old." He shoved a hand in his pocket. "I know a fellow GenXer when I see one."

Was he flirting with me? Or was he trying to charm me into saying something stupid or incriminating? "My father was a police officer, an investigator for most of his career. He taught me a lot about how to work a crime scene."

"Was?"

"He died over a decade ago."

"On the job?"

I shook my head. "Heart."

"Ah." He gave me a solemn nod. "According to Copper, he taught you well. Your quick thinking is the only reason we have any part of the scene preserved."

"Oh, good. He was able to get her covered before the storm got too crazy."

A shout of anger interrupted our conversation. The chief and I both pivoted to observe the confrontation. It was Paul and Blake, Darlene's fiancé, shoving each other while a guy I recognized as the drummer from the night before pushed them apart. I guess the band was back together again.

"Excuse me, Ms. Black. I think I need to go slap some

idiots." He tapped the edge of his wide-brimmed hat. "I'll be right back."

After the chief walked away, I gestured for my friends to join me.

"Well?" Gilly asked. "Are we free to go?"

"Almost," I told her. "Just have to give our statements."

"What's happening over there?" Tippi gestured to the fighting men.

"If I had to guess, Paul is pissed off at the world that his sister is dead, and he's laying blame on anyone he can to avoid his own guilt."

"Guilt for what?" the younger Davenport inquired.

"For whatever. When someone we love dies suddenly, it's hard not to think about all the would've, should've, could'ves." I had regrets after my dad died. It had been three weeks since I'd called him. I'd been busy preparing for a presentation for a new client, and I never imagined that I wouldn't be able to speak to him again. I was so angry at the world for snatching him away from me. "The anger will fade." And then the pain would really hit him hard.

The chief broke up the fight, sending Paul back to the winery. The bearded guy had his arm around Blake, whose tear-streaked face was as red as Pinot Noir. Copper went over and started talking to them. Another golf cart parked at the end of the row, and Donna got out and trotted down the aisle to her mother.

Hail, hail the gang's all here.

70

Donna and Rhonda put their heads together. I didn't like the way they kept looking over at us or the way Donna had pointed at Tippi.

"Why does she keep looking at me like that?" Tippi brushed her hand over the front of her shirt as if another drink had been thrown at her.

Pippa looped her arm with Tippi's at the elbow. "Just ignore them. By evening, we'll be back home in our own beds, and this whole terrible day will be a memory." She looked at me. "So to speak."

Rhonda signaled for Chief Porter.

Uh oh. Not good.

"What do you think she's telling him?" Gilly's tone was pinched. "I mean, there's nothing, right? We don't even know these people."

"We're about to find out," I told her when the chief started our way.

"Ms. Davenport, can you account for your whereabouts last night after you left La Sous Terre?" he asked.

"She was at the cabin with us," Pippa answered. "All night."

"I'm afraid I'm going to need to hear that from Ms. Davenport."

"I...my sister told you, I was at the cabin."

"I have an eyewitness who saw you jogging on the road last night near the vineyards around eight o'clock in the evening. Do you want to amend your statement?"

Pippa looked dumbstruck. "I forgot about that. Tippi

just went out for a little run to clear her head. She wasn't gone long."

Tippi had been gone for almost two hours, but I wasn't going to volunteer the information.

The chief was undeterred as he questioned Tippi further. "Do you have anyone who can account for the time you were out?"

I liked to believe that the police were competent, even in small towns like Marseille, but I was beginning to worry about where this was heading. "Does Tippi need a lawyer?"

"Right now, we're just having a friendly chat," he answered. "But if you think she needs a lawyer, I'm perfectly happy to take this interview down to the station."

Nothing about the "interview" felt friendly. "Tippi? Did you see anyone on your run?"

She shook her head. "I ran for about forty minutes, then..."

"Then what?" the chief asked. "Did you see Darlene?"

"No," Tippi denied. "I jogged to the First Christian Church off Palmer Road. It's past the vineyard about a mile."

Pippa tucked her chin and frowned. "You went to church?"

Tippi sucked her teeth with obvious exasperation. "For a meeting," she admitted. "I went to an AA meeting at the church. I'd called my sponsor, and she'd found me a local place to go. I was there for another forty minutes. Then I went back to the cabin."

"Can anyone vouch for you?" the chief asked.

"It's anonymous for a reason. I might be able to point out someone there, but we don't do last names in Alcoholics Anonymous and half the time, the first names are made up. Besides, I didn't speak to anyone."

Poor Tippi. It had cost her to admit that she'd been struggling bad enough to need a meeting.

"I'm proud of you," I told her. "You took care of yourself."

She gave me a tight smile.

"Well, until we can find someone to corroborate your story or we get another suspect, I'm going to need you all to stick around for a few more days. As it stands, I still need your statements about today. I'll send Copper over to record them."

He stalked off and joined his investigators as they were putting up the party canopy. The sky had mostly cleared off, but I understood why they didn't want to take any chances on the weather shifting again.

Once he was out of earshot, Gilly whined, "Nooooo. I can't stick around for a few days. I need to be home by Friday. I am not going to be late for my own wedding." She pivoted her gaze to our youngest companion. "Sorry, Tipster. We know you didn't do it. They'll find the killer, and all will be well." Then my BFF of fifty years whipped her gaze to mine. "Right, Nora?"

"You made me promise to stay out of it."

"And now I'm asking you to break it. We are on a mission. Operation Get Gilly Married is in full effect."

"Hey," Tippi complained. "What about Operation Exonerate Tippi?

Gilly looked chagrinned but unfettered. "It's a double mission." She took my hands. "Do you accept?"

I squeezed her hands and locked gazes with her. "I do."

"Then get to sniffing, or whatever it is you need to do, so we can save my..." She made a face at Tippi. "So, we can save my friend." Out the side of her mouth, she added, "And my nuptials."

"In that order," I told her. But first, I was going to make a call to a certain hot detective I knew. If I wanted to keep my second promise, I was going to need all the help I could get.

CHAPTER

EIGHT

B ack at the cabin, Gilly went into her bedroom and started the hot water filling the giant tub. "I'll be out when the water is cold," she told us, then shut the door behind her.

I'd called Ezra on the drive from the winery, and he told me to sit tight until he called back with whatever information he could find out. So, sitting tight was exactly what I planned to do. For now.

Pippa dropped her bag on a dining room chair. "This is so bad. So, so bad."

"I didn't do it," Tippi stated.

"Of course, you didn't," I told her.

"I have to call Jordy. I need to hear his voice." She made a brisk exit to her room, leaving me alone with our own red herring. I smiled reassuringly at Tippi. "Having a drink tossed on you is not a motive for murder. Chief Porter isn't a stupid man." At least, I hoped he wasn't.

"He's just covering all his bases. He'll cross you off the list and move on."

"Until then, where do we start our investigation?" Tippi asked.

"We?" I gave her a dubious stare.

She batted her blue eyes at me. "I'm a suspect in the murder of a woman I don't even know. Of course, I want to help."

"You can help by staying out of it. If you get involved, it's only going to make you look more suspicious."

"Ah." She nodded as she tied her hair back into a ponytail. "You mean because criminals like to insert themselves into their own cases as a way to show how clever they are."

"You watch too much television." I took a can of coffee from the shelf to the right of the stove and ladled a couple of scoops into the filter basket above the pot.

"I don't watch hardly any TV," she said. "But I do listen to a lot of true crime podcasts. I feel like it makes me an expert."

I snorted a laugh as I filled the pot with water and then dumped it into the back of the coffee maker. "On what?" I asked. "Listening to people talk about murder? That's not a helpful investigation tool."

"I know all the tricks of the trade," she said. "I can get into the killer's mind."

I slipped the pot into its cradle and turned on the

machine before raising my gaze to Tippi. "You realize you're not helping your case."

"It's not like I was going to tell the police that I'm a murder expert. That would be stupid."

"You're right, of course," I said with an eye roll. "How foolish of me to assume." I pushed her my phone. "If you want to be helpful, you can search for anything you can find out about Darlene Nichols and the rest of her dysfunctional family. Oh, and find out more about the boyfriend as well."

"I have my own phone." She pushed mine back across the counter.

I slid it back to her. "Yes, but my phone is less likely to be subpoenaed."

"Smart!" She snapped her fingers. "You are really good at this."

"Thanks. I'm not a podcast expert, but..." I spread my hands as I let the implication lay in the air.

"You're kind of being a dick," she told me. Her eyes widened, and she put her hand over her mouth. "I'm sorry. I didn't mean to call you a dick."

I laughed. "I've been called worse, and I am being a little bit of a dick." I tapped my phone screen. "Even so, a little more information would be really helpful."

"Fine," she said. "I'll be guided by the wisdom of my elders."

I picked up a dishtowel and threw it at her. "You're a brat."

She laughed as she sidestepped the flying terrycloth. "You're not wrong."

AN HOUR HAD PASSED, then two. What was keeping Ezra? I was a patient woman, but I could only look at the river for so long before I started getting a little stir-crazy. I'd promised Gilly that I'd get her home on time for her to become Mrs. Scott Graham. Well, she was keeping her last name this time, but the sentiment was the same. She'd found love again, and that was rare. I'll admit there was a childish part of me that fantasized about Gilly staying single and the two of us growing old together, two old crones against the world. But that child could suck it. The better part of me, the part that wanted all the happiness in the world for my best friend, was going to move Heaven and Earth to make sure Gilly got that happiness she so much deserved.

But sitting on the back porch waiting for my guy to call with news felt like the antithesis of that hope and dream. When Tippi finished her web crawl and gave me back my phone, I texted Ezra for the fourth time since our last call.

Anything? I'm getting antsy.

There were some bouncing ellipses, then nothing. Come on, Ezra, I thought. Come through for me. Maybe he was having trouble accessing an old database. Or maybe he'd gotten caught using police resources to help his girlfriend and was in trouble. Or maybe there just wasn't anything to find.

Hah. This family was volatile. There's no way none of them had a record. Or at least a few arrests. Also, the jury was still out for me on whether Chief Porter was competent or not.

According to Tippi's research, the chief had worked in St. Louis as a police officer for fifteen years before moving to Marseille to take the job as chief. He'd held the job for the past twelve years. She couldn't find any unsavory news. He had a low digital footprint and no social media that she could find. Now she was scouring the web for dirt on the Nichols family. So far, the search had been a bust.

I glanced down at my phone. The ellipses had stopped bouncing, and a new text never arrived.

Hello? Didn't get your text.

There was a knock at the front door. Probably Rhonda Nichols, serving us an eviction notice. *Nah.* I got the impression that the woman liked money too much to kick us out.

I peeked out the spyhole and felt a whoosh go through my body as I flung the door open. Ezra stood on the porch, wearing shorts that hugged his hips, a sage green tank top that showed off his broad shoulders and muscled arms, and white tennis shoes that didn't detract from the rest of his hotness. Jordy and Scott were behind him on the front stoop, all three of them with overnight bags in hand.

Ezra's green eyes sparkled as he dipped his head to kiss me. "I don't text and drive."

"Get in here," I told them. "I can't believe you drove all this way."

"You sounded like you could use some backup," Ezra said.

"And there was no way we were getting left behind," Jordy added. He jerked his thumb at Scott. "And wild horses weren't keeping Doc from coming along."

I frowned at Ezra's pale legs. "Cute legs," I told him.

"Appropriate for a fishing trip," he replied.

Well, poop. I'd forgotten that today was the day Ezra and Jordy had planned guy stuff for Scott. "I'm sorry you had to cancel your plans."

He pressed his forehead to mine. "But you're not sorry I'm here."

"Definitely not sorry about that." I hadn't worked any cases without him, and having a special investigator in our midst would make it harder for the local PD to run roughshod over Tippi.

"Jordy," I heard Tippi say, then Pippa's door flung open, and she rushed out into the living room to greet her husband.

Scott looked around. "Where's Gilly?"

"She's sulking in her room." I pointed to the door closest to the balcony.

He made a beeline to the room and went inside, closing the door behind him. I heard a squawk of surprise and then a squeal of delight, followed by a splash. I looped my arms around Ezra's neck. "All's right with the world for a minute."

Jordy, Pippa, and Tippi went out to the deck, leaving Ezra and me alone.

I gave him another kiss. "You didn't have to come, but I'm so glad you did."

He smirked. "I haven't come yet, but I can always add it to the agenda."

I laughed. "You're so bad."

"As the old saying goes, when I'm good, I'm very good." He pressed his body against mine and kissed me in a way that made my toes curl. His lips moved from my mouth to my ear, and he added, "But when I'm bad, I'm better."

"Okay, Mae West," I teased, but honestly, I hadn't realized how much tension I was holding until now. "I'm so glad you're here."

He brushed my hair from my face with his fingers. "I didn't need much of an excuse. Next time, skip the dead body and just ask."

"Hah." I patted his chest. "I'll make a note." Sighing, I rested my cheek against his chest. "Speaking of the dead body. Did you find out anything?"

"I gave the list of names you asked me to look up to Shawn, and he's supposed to call if he finds something."

"My ex?"

"My chief," Ezra corrected. "But, yes, also your ex." He chuckled. "I had to call him to get a few days extra off from work, and he offered to help. He has a lot of respect for you."

I nodded. "It's mutual."

Shawn Rafferty and I had been high school sweethearts, married in college, and divorced by the time we were twenty-five. Irreconcilable differences. I didn't want children, and he did. Even so, our breakup had been amicable, with neither of us asking for anything more than an equal split of assets. Now, we were friends of a sort, and I liked having him back in my life. Even more, I liked his wife, the mother of his two children.

Shawn and I had both gotten what we'd wanted in life, just not from each other, and that was okay. If we'd stayed together, one of us—more likely both of us—would've ended up miserable, full of resentment and anger. Now, I worked as a consultant for the Garden Cove Police Department, and I'd been instrumental in helping Ezra and Shawn solve a few bad cases.

I loved the man holding me in his arms, and I loved my life. More so, I loved not worrying about what happened next.

Ezra took my hand as we went into the kitchen area. I poured us both a cup of coffee, stirring a spoonful of sugar into his cup.

I set it down in front of him on the breakfast counter, then leaned forward onto my elbows. "This has been a weird two days."

"Walk me through it," he said. "From the beginning, and don't leave out anything. Including any visions you might've experienced."

I wasn't sure the memories I'd witnessed were related to the death. Just a lot of hanky-panky in storage spaces. However, Darlene had been a witness to the one in the wine cellar, so it could be relevant. "Okay," I told Ezra. "But it's about to get spicy."

"All right then," he quipped. "Bring the heat."

CHAPTER
NINE

"Booze and sex," Ezra mused. "As they say in wine country, they pair together well."

I groaned at the bad joke. "Har har." I'd told him about the beer spill in some kind of storage closet and the wine breakage in the cellar, along with everything I'd overheard last night when Tippi and I were in the bathroom. Shawn still hadn't called with any new information. Ezra put his phone down on the counter between us, so he wouldn't miss it when it came.

"Oh." I'd almost forgotten about Donna's petty behavior at the wine shop. "Donna Patterson, Rhonda's daughter, got real snide with Paul right before the tour."

"Paul's the nephew, the victim's brother?"

"Yep." I took a sip of my coffee. It had cooled some, but it was still satisfying. "Donna taunted him about her mother inheriting the vineyard and not him. I'm also pretty sure she's the one who pointed the finger at Tippi.

Which begs the question, what was she doing when she saw Tip out for a run?"

"You know what?" Ezra's brow quirked up. "I think this situation calls for a murder board."

Gilly exited the bedroom, dressed in flowy black yoga pants and a flared, short-sleeved top. Her hair was wrapped in a towel. "Did someone say murder board?"

Scott, who Gilly always thought looked a bit like Harrison Ford, trailed after her, now in jeans and a t-shirt. His damp hair and five o'clock shadow were definitely giving off some Indiana Jones vibes, and it didn't take an archeologist to figure out that he had found her Temple of Womb. He carried his wet shorts and shirt to the deck and hung them over a lounge chair.

Pippa said from the deck, "Oooo, a murder board! We've never done one of those."

My excitement mirrored theirs. I'd only read about murder boards or seen them in my favorite cozy mysteries on television. The board consisted of a victim portrait, suspects, locations, motives, opportunities, alibis, and anything else that might be pertinent to a case. On the one hand, someone had to die for a murder board to exist, which was terrible. On the other hand... murder board!

I scanned the room. "We need something large that we can hang up and write on. Does anyone have a marker?"

"They have a Dollar General in town," Pippa said. "Jordy and I can do a supply run."

"And me!" Tippi raised her hand to volunteer.

"No," Gilly, Pippa, and I said in stereo.

Ezra chuckled. "Tip, it's probably better if you stay put for now. Out of sight, out of mind, and all that."

"Fine." She harumphed and flopped onto the couch. "But it's not fair. I didn't do anything."

"Some people are born trouble-magnets," Jordy teased. Jordy's long hair was pulled back and piled on his head in a messy man-bun, exposing the tattoos on his neck. He had ink down both arms, his chest, and his neck. Memories for him, some he cherished, and some he'd rather forget. I knew the feeling. Several tats on his arms were to cover old needle scars from heavy drug use. I noticed he had tattoos peeking out from below his shorts.

I peered at him. "I don't think I've ever seen your legs."

He turned his ankle and struck a pose. "Sexy, huh?"

Pippa giggled as she smacked him with the back of her hand.

"Dead sexy." I laughed.

Ezra got in on the action. "But not as sexy as mine, right?"

"Nope, not as sexy as yours." I grinned at Jordy. "No offense."

"Whatever." He flicked his finger under his chin. "Come on, Pip. Let's go where I'll be more appreciated."

I snickered. "The Dollar General?"

"Money is always appreciated." He laced his fingers in Pippa's as they headed out.

I leaned forward to put myself closer to Ezra. "I can't believe we're doing a murder board. I don't think you've ever been sexier."

"If I had known how much you wanted one, I'd have put one up in my bedroom a long time ago."

"Okay, ew," Tippi complained from the couch. "Take your weird sex talk to another room."

I gave Ezra a coy smile and softly said, "You know all the right things to say to push my buttons."

Gilly plopped down next to Ezra. "Tell me all about these right things you say to Nora. I'm sure we'd all love to hear."

Tippi placed a throw pillow over her face. "No, we wouldn't," came her muffled protest. She removed the pillow and stared at us. "Some of us get no sexy talk, and we certainly don't want to have to listen to it."

Tippi had been single since she'd arrived in Garden Cove. The first year had been part of her sobriety plan, but since then, there'd been no other reason for her to stay celibate than fear. She told me once that she'd never had sex with someone when she wasn't drunk. Her confession made me sad for her.

Gilly clucked at her. "Speak for yourself."

Tippi tossed the throw pillow in our general direction. "I am!"

"Okay," I interjected. "Let's all settle down."

Ezra's phone lit up, rang, and danced a little as it

vibrated against the granite counter. "Saved by the bell." He snatched it up to answer. "Hey, Chief. I'm putting you on speaker. I have Nora, Gilly, Scott, and Tippi here."

"Scott?" Shawn asked.

"Doctor Graham. The emergency room doctor at the hospital."

"Who's hurt?" Shawn sounded worried.

"He's Gilly's fiancé," I chirped in. "He's not here professionally."

"I'd like to think I'm more than my job," Scott murmured.

Gilly gave his butt a pinch. "Definitely more," she told him.

He smiled, mollified.

"Right. Of course," Shawn said quickly. "Layla mentioned she was getting married. Congratulations, Gilly."

"Thanks, Shawn," Gilly said loudly.

"Did you find out anything useful?" I asked.

"Nora Black," Shawn muttered. "Always down to business."

His surly tone raised my hackles, but he was helping us out, so I tried not to match his energy. "I appreciate you agreeing to help. You didn't have to, so thank you."

My thanks took some of the wind out of his sails. "Terry Porter seems to be a stand-up cop. No red flags that I could find. I called a buddy in St. Louis who used to work with him. He said Porter liked the ladies, but otherwise, he had been as straight-laced as they come."

88

"He likes the ladies," I conceded.

Ezra gave me a questioning look.

"I'm pretty sure he's sleeping with Rhonda Nichols, and he was flirting with me last night and a little bit today. At least, that's the way it felt."

My guy's lips thinned into a grim line. He had to know he had nothing to worry about. Regardless of what Gilly had said in the past about me having a type, it wasn't true. I fell for Shawn before he was a cop, and other than Shawn, the only other police officer I ever went with was Ezra. Most of the men I'd dated were professional businessmen. Even so, I was happy on my current journey and in love with my traveling companion.

"What about the Nichols? Anything on that family?" I asked.

"No convictions. Though, there is a Matilda Carson who was arrested for embezzlement. The charges were dropped by Thomas Nichols. The report says she is the complainant's sister."

"That has to be Ellie's mom. She's a first cousin to Paul and Darlene, and Tommy Nichols was her uncle. She says her mom works for a bank in town as their bookkeeper and that she used to keep the books for the vineyards."

Gilly's gaze found me. "Do you think she was embezzling?"

"When was the report?" I asked Shawn.

"Nineteen Ninety-nine," he replied.

"That's three years before Jonathan Nichols died and left the business to Thomas."

"How do you know all this?" Shawn asked incredulously.

"People like to talk, and I like to listen," I said.

Gilly snorted. "And she asks a lot of questions."

"I have a curious mind."

"I can't remember what I had for breakfast," Scott said. "I don't know how you keep it all in your head."

I hadn't thought of it before, but since gaining my aroma-mojo for other people's memories, *my* memory had started improving. I mean, it had never been terrible, but I'd noticed in my forties that little things would slip my mind. Now, it was almost like I had perfect recall. Maybe my sixth sense had more benefits beyond seeing visions of the past. "I don't know how I do it either," I mused. "It's something I'll need to think over."

Ezra's brow quirked.

I shook my head. We could talk about it later. Right now, the focus was getting as much information as possible to point the finger at someone other than Tippi so we could all go home.

"Why would her brother falsely accuse her?" Tippi asked.

"Inheritance," I stated. "From my one vision of Thomas Nichols, he seemed like a bit of a control freak. Not the kind of guy who wants to share the reins with someone else."

The door opened. Jordy and Pippa walked in,

holding two small yellow bags and one large white-board. "We're back. And let me tell you, the Dollar General is huge. It even has a real grocery side. Anyhow, we got the murder board!"

"Murder board?" Shawn's tone held many, many questions.

Pippa's eyes widened when I pointed to the phone.

She mouthed, "Yikes," then or "Hello, Chief Rafferty. This is Pippa Hines. I was just kidding."

"No, she wasn't," I told him. "We're making a murder board."

He paused momentarily, and no one spoke while we waited for his response. Finally, he said, "Damn, now I'm jealous."

We all laughed a little, our relief palpable.

"Where were we?" I gestured to Pippa to get the board set up.

She took it from Jordy and pressed the back against the refrigerator. To my surprise, it stuck.

"It's magnetic," Pippa beamed. Jordy handed her a dry-erase marker. "Can I do the honors?"

"Go for it." I circled my hand at her. "Make a list of all the players."

She nodded, marker at the ready. "Do it."

"Chief Porter. On the surface, he's on the up and up, but he's got a reputation as a ladies' man. Possibly having an affair with the victim's aunt."

Pippa wrote:

Chief Porter
> *Up and up?*
> *Ladies' man*
> *Affair with aunt?*

"Okay," Pippa said. "Next."

"Thomas Nichols accused his sister, Matilda Carson, of embezzlement in 1999," Gilly told her.

"What does that have to do with the current crime?" Pippa asked.

"We don't know," I said honestly. "But I'm pretty sure she's Ellie's mom, so maybe it's relevant, maybe it's not. Old grudges die hard."

Pippa dug in. "But wouldn't the grudge be against the previous owner, Thomas Nichols, or even the wife, Rhonda?"

"We don't have to make sense of it yet. Let's just catalog what we know," I suggested.

"Fine," she agreed. "But I'm putting Matilda under Ellie."

Ellie (Cousin)
> *Works Corked*
> *Mom accused of embezzlement*
> *Upset about victim's death*

"She looked upset before the tour," I added. "The blonde we saw storming around the back of the shop. I'm pretty sure it was her."

"I really thought that was Darlene," Tippi commented.

Pippa added:

Upset prior to discovery of body.

"Who's next?" Shawn asked over the speaker. Garden Cove must've been experiencing a tiresome week because he sounded downright giddy.

"You tell me," I told him. "Did you find anything on anyone else?"

"Darlene Nichols had one arrest for drunk and disorderly," he told us. "But it was dismissed."

"That's a shocker," Tippi scoffed. She reddened at her outburst. "Sorry. I know she's the victim here, but she was kind of awful."

Darlene Nichols (Victim)
    Alcoholic?
    Jealous
    Angry
    A wild card
    Didn't get along with aunt
    Engaged to cheater

She wasn't a suspect in her own crime, but it didn't hurt to have what we knew about her on the board.

"Let's look at Rhonda Nichols next." I tapped my chin. "She married Thomas Nichols two years after his wife died. The wife died seven years ago, which means they were married for five years. From what I have gathered, she inherited the entire family estate, all the money and the business."

"You're kidding," Ezra stated.

"Not in the least. Thomas Nichols only died three months ago, and I think Darlene and maybe Paul were looking for a way to contest the will."

Pippa continued adding information to the board.

Rhonda Nichols
> _Gold-digger?_
> _Disliked victim_
> _Husband died recently_
> _Inherited everything_
> _Possible affair with COP_

"Cop?" Ezra asked.

"Chief of Police," Pippa explained. "I abbreviated it to take up less room."

"Ah." He gave her a quick two-finger salute. "Got it."

"Paul Nichols, the victim's brother, seemed genuinely upset when we found her."

"I imagine so," Scott said gravely.

"What about Blake Perkins?" Tippi asked. "The cheating fiancé."

"I did find one report on him," Shawn said. "He was arrested for assault and battery four years ago."

"Was it a domestic?" I asked him. "Was he violent with Darlene?"

"I can't attest to that," Shawn told us. "But the fight happened at a bar. Some place called Night Owls."

"Who did he get in a fight with?"

Shawn made a grunting noise. "Connor Copper."

I dropped my hands to my side. "The police officer?"

"Is he?" Shawn asked.

"Yes, he is," I affirmed. "And he was the first one on the scene."

CHAPTER

TEN

"This doesn't make any sense," I said. "Officer Copper told me he knew of the family but wasn't a friend. He told me that Darlene was a few years ahead of him in school, and Paul was well out of high school while he was still in elementary."

"Unless Copper's fight with Blake had nothing to do with Darlene or the Nichols. Maybe he was just in the wrong place at the wrong time," Jordy supposed. "It's happened to me a time or two."

"And there would be no reason for him to disclose that to you, Nora," Shawn's voice said over the speaker. "After all, Blake wasn't the victim."

"True." Unfortunately, I didn't know any players well enough to know what might have motivated the killing. "For all we know," I said aloud. "It might not be any of them. Maybe it was a crime of opportunity."

"Oh, gosh." Tippi put her hand to her mouth. "You don't think she was raped, do you?"

I shrugged. "It's a possibility. All we saw was her face and left arm. She had fingertip bruises around her biceps like someone had grabbed her hard."

"She also had on a ring that had to have cost several grand," Pippa remarked. "And it was still on her finger."

"So, it wasn't a robbery," Ezra surmised.

Pippa was scribbling fast and furious on the whiteboard as we threw out ideas.

"I feel sick." Tippi got up and went out to the back deck. "I need some air." Tippi hadn't liked Darlene, but she wouldn't have wished this on her.

Pippa gave Jordy a pointed look. He gave her a curt nod. "I'll check on her."

The line between Pippa's brow relaxed as she nodded to Jordy. "Thank you."

"Who are we missing?" Ezra asked. "We've talked about Porter, Rhonda, Paul, Ellie, Blake, and Copper. Is that it?"

"Donna," I said. "Donna is Rhonda's daughter. There's no love lost between her and Paul. I can't imagine her relationship with Darlene was any better. She was smug about Paul being cut out of the will and wasn't bashful about airing the information in front of strangers."

"Hmm." Ezra tugged at his ear and then scratched his brow. "You got anything else for us, chief?"

"Nothing too revelatory. Paul Nichols got a speeding ticket in St. Louis about a month ago, but otherwise, nothing on paper." Shawn cleared his throat. "I can call Porter and tell him a little about how you've helped Garden Cove with some cases. He might be inclined to let you in."

"Do you honestly believe that?"

"No," Shawn answered. "But I would do it."

I smiled. "And I appreciate it, but no. At least for right now. Who knows, you may be getting a call from me later."

"I'd like that," he said. "Easy, keep me informed of what's going on."

"You got it, Chief," Ezra said. "I'll text you with any new information."

There was another pause. "You guys really have a murder board?"

I chuckled when Pippa exclaimed, "We sure do."

"Talk soon." Shawn ended the call.

Gilly leaned against Scott but focused her stare at me. "Well, that was kind of a bust."

"I don't know about that." I tried to sound reassuring. "We've got more information than we had before."

Ezra put his hand on mine. "I think it's time we went sniffing around. See if we can get your nose on the case."

"I'm on board for the plan. I think we should start at the wine shop first."

"What about us?" Gilly asked. "Can we do anything?"

Ezra got up from his perch on the stool. "Asking

questions isn't against the law. Why don't you and Scott go to the bar Night Owls and see if anyone remembers Blake and Copper's fight, and even if they don't, see if they know Blake or Darlene? Getting some history from non-family members might give a more accurate depiction of their relationship."

"You think he could've killed her?" Pippa asked.

Ezra turned his palms up as he spread his hands. "From what Ellie told Nora, Darlene talked about breaking her engagement again. Maybe she did, and maybe Blake got mad enough to hurt her. It's not a stretch as far as motive goes."

Pippa seemed to consider the idea for a moment, then nodded. "What can I do?"

I gave my friend an apologetic frown. "I hate to say this, but I think you should stay here with Tippi. She needs to stay put, and if we leave her alone, I don't think she will."

Jordy came back inside. "What are we doing?"

"Nora and Ezra are handing out assignments." Pippa's tone was sullen.

"What can I do?" Jordy asked.

"You're an unknown around here," Ezra told him. "And you know how to listen when people gossip."

Jordy walked over to his wife and put his arm over her shoulder. "I serve coffee all day. I can't help it if people want to treat my place of business like a confessional. It's not like I'm asking a bunch of nosey questions."

"You have a face that people want to confide in, babe," Pippa cooed. "It's one of the many reasons I fell in love with you."

"All right." Jordy's eyes flared with affection. "I'll poke a few hornets' nests and see what comes out."

"If it's a mass of hornets, run," Pippa told him.

"Like the wind, my love." He took her hand and kissed her fingertips. "Like the wind."

THE LATE-AFTERNOON SKY was blue except for a few fluffy white clouds. Other than some downed tree limbs and a few puddles that the bright sunshine hadn't dried yet, there wasn't any trace of the earlier Stormaggedon. Ezra and I got out of my car in the parking lot at the Rivière Tranquille store. I saw Jordy get out of Ezra's truck at the end of the lot. He'd changed into jeans before we'd left, but he still stuck out like a sore thumb.

"Do you think this was the mission for Jordy?"

"He has the tattoos of a scary biker but the face of an angel." Ezra grinned. "He'll do fine. People like him."

"He's easy to like," I admitted. "But maybe we like him because we know him. Just saying."

Ezra chuckled, and the low timbre of his voice sent a thrill through me. "We got to know him because we liked him."

"Maybe you're right."

"I'll mark it down in the books."

I gave his shoulder a playful punch.

He laughed again. "You know I like it when you get rough."

"Stop it." I stifled a giggle as I reached for the front door. "We need to blend in." I turned the handle, but the door didn't budge. "It's locked." I groaned. "I didn't even think... Of course, they're closed. They just had a death in the family, and their vineyard is a crime scene."

I saw Jordy going around back toward the fields. "Why don't we see if the winery is open? That place is full of things that stink."

"After you." Ezra urged me ahead of him.

"You know, I could tell that Paul cares about this place. He went to school to become a wine scientist. This vineyard is in his blood, literally."

Ezra put his hand on my back as we walked up four concrete steps behind the store. "What are you thinking?"

"I don't get why Thomas would've cut them out of the inheritance. According to Ellie, Thomas and his wife Jen practically raised Paul and Darlene. On top of that, he was so adamant about tradition in the vision I had of him with Paul. Would a man like that let this place go to someone who isn't a blood relative?"

"It's hard to fathom but not impossible. Spite makes people do all kinds of things they wouldn't normally do."

I gave Ezra a sideways glance. "What has spite made you do?"

"For one, I acted like my mother didn't exist for years. I let spite get in the way of having a relationship with her until now."

It was true. Even when we'd met, I'd thought his mother was dead. To find out she wasn't had been surprising. "I get it," I told him as we crossed the short distance to the large industrial barn-looking building with all the crushing machines and fermenting vats. "I'm sure I've done or said things out of spite as well." I pointed. "That's where the wine is made."

"I don't believe you've ever been spiteful," Ezra said. "You're the kindest, least judgmental person I know."

"I'm sure Gilly could drum up a few stories if you need proof that I can be as petty as the next person." Still, his compliment made me smile. "But thank you."

"You don't have to thank me for telling the truth." Ezra tested the door. It easily opened. He winked at me. "It looks like we're in business."

"Let's just hope this doesn't end with both of us arrested for trespassing. Gilly won't forgive me if I'm in jail on her wedding day."

Ezra grinned. "Then we better not get caught."

ELEVEN

"I thought there would be more noise. Whirring. Crunching. Beeping." Ezra wrinkled his nose. "It smells sweet and tart in here. It's kind of making me hungry."

"Have you eaten today?"

"I was busy getting my butt on the road." He gave me a 'duh' look. "And if you think it was easy getting Jordy and Scott to hurry, you don't know them very well. Those two have no sense of urgency."

I squinted at him. "That's surprising considering Scott works in the emergency room where urgency is literally required."

"Well, it doesn't translate to his personal life. The guy is a turtle."

"He won the race for Gilly's heart," I pointed out. "I guess he doesn't need to be any faster than that."

Ezra shook his head and smiled. "Fair point." Then

he smacked me on the butt. "Okay, woman, get to sniffin'."

"You're going to pay for that later."

"If I'm real lucky."

I strolled near the crusher contraption. "This is where the grapes are pulverized, and the juice is strained into a big receptacle underneath. The skins and any other solid stuff are tossed if it's white grapes and mixed in if it's red." I took a whiff inside the top of the machine. The aroma was slightly acidic but not overpowering. "Nothing here," I told him.

I moved on to the chiller unit. There was a slight hum, indicating the power was on. "Paul said there aren't any wines in the early stages right now, but I think they keep the chiller on year-round." There was a presence of ozone and metal in the air. I concentrated, trying to find any emotion related to an industrial scent, but again, I came up empty-handed.

I gave Ezra a flat look. "If I didn't want to have a vision, I'd be hit with five, and now that I want one, nothing is happening."

He nodded. "Let's go into the next room."

"That's the fermentation room." The heavy metal door was on a spring hinge that automatically closed when you let go. There were lights on the machines that cast a dim glow, but otherwise, it was hard to see around the space. It was a warm room, but the fermentation tanks felt cool when my arm brushed one. According to

Paul, they weren't in use this time of year, but I could still detect the faint odor of tart grapes.

"This has promise," Ezra said.

"Yeah, but for what? I feel like we are looking for a needle in a pile of needles." I moved carefully around the room. Trying not to trip over anything, I inhaled deeply and caught the stringent odor of orange peels from a large wooden crate. "Wait, what's..."

A blast of thunder shakes the building as a figure ducks inside the room. The rain pelting on the metal roof is loud and unnerving. They are covered, head to toe, in a rain suit. Gray like the one Chief Porter had been wearing, but this one is larger, less fitting.

The face is a blur, as always with my visions, and I can't make out hair color, length, or style since they have the hood up and pulled tightly around their face. The person has on gloves, and they're holding something. It's too hard to see what it is in the dim light, but I hear a clank as they toss it behind a box near the fermentation barrels.

Without stopping, the figure dashes from the room.

I blinked as the vision faded. "That was strange," I said.

"What did you see?"

"Not a lot, but an intense emotion was attached to the vision. It was pure, unadulterated panic." I pointed behind a crate of dried orange peels. "Whatever the person was trying to dispose of, it's back there."

"Dispose of?"

"Hide is maybe a better word," I told him. "I think it happened during the storm this afternoon."

Ezra clicked a mini flashlight attached to his key ring and pointed it behind the case. He leaned over, coming off one leg, to get a closer look. "I see something," he said. "It's shiny."

"Careful," I warned. My heart picked up the pace. "It could be a knife or a gun or a needle full of drugs or poison."

Ezra turned his chin over his shoulder to look at me. "I'm not going to grab it with my bare hands. I'm only trying to identify it."

"Yep, okay. That sounds like a good plan."

"I'm glad you approve." He sounded amused. "I'm going to slide these crates out." There was a *maaawww* sound of wood being dragged a few inches across the rough concrete floor. Ezra stopped tugging on them. "Damn, these are heavier than I thought."

"Can I help?" I got on the other side of the crate, and between us, we moved the box a few feet away from the wall and fermentation vat.

Ezra and I squatted for a closer look. The beam on his light wasn't powerful enough to capture the entire object all at once.

"What is that?" Ezra said. "It looks coiled."

"I think it's a bottle opener."

The ceiling light flickered on. "Someone's coming." My pulse began to race again. "We have to get out of here." This wasn't an official investigation. Neither of us had permission to be on the property, and I didn't want to spend the night in jail for trespassing.

"I can't leave," Ezra intoned.

The flight in my fight-or-flight was strong. I briefly entertained the notion of fleeing without him but brushed it away. I was a scrapper, and if we had to fight, I would, but Gilly would kill me if I had a black eye or broken nose in her wedding pictures. My love for Ezra outweighed my fear of Gilly. "Why can't we leave?"

"Because this corkscrew has blood on it."

Well, crap on toast. The corkscrew had a carved mahogany handle with the letters R and T engraved into the top. The wicked-looking screw attached at the center appeared thicker in diameter than most of the ones I had seen. There were dark brown stains on the metal and a smear of ruddy red on the pale concrete below it.

"What if it's only wine?"

"What if it's not?" His expression was apologetic. "If this is evidence, I can't abandon it."

"What if the person who turned on the lights is the killer?"

"We have the element of surprise." Ezra got up, put his back to the wall next to the door, and gestured for me to do the same on the other side of the door. "When they come through, I'll subdue them, and you call for help."

I didn't love the plan, but I nodded my agreement.

The handle jiggled, and there was a squeak as the door slowly opened.

Chief Terry Porter walked inside with Connor Copper right behind him. I shook my head at Ezra. The situation had just gone from bad to worse. We were toast.

Running wasn't an option. One, I wasn't fast enough to get away on foot, and two, see number one.

"Hello, Chief," I said.

Both officers nearly jumped out of their skin as they whipped around to face me. Copper had his hand on his holstered pistol.

I raised my hands. "Don't shoot."

"Ms. Black, what in the world are you doing in here?" He glanced Ezra's way. "And who's your friend?"

Ezra turned on his one-hundred-watt smile and used what I like to call his "good ol' boy" voice. "Detective Ezra Holden." He held out his hand. "Garden Cove Police. I head up the special investigations."

"You're a long way from home, Detective," Porter observed unhappily. "Why are you here?"

"He's my partner," I blurted.

"I thought you said you were a soap maker." The chief narrowed his gaze on me. "Why would you lie about being in law enforcement?"

"I *am* a soap maker. I also make lotions and body sprays, but that's not the point. Ezra's my...uhm, life partner." We had to find a better word for our relationship. The partner thing, with him being a cop, tended to throw people off. "You know, my..."

"Her main squeeze," Ezra filled in.

If the situation hadn't been dire, I might have laughed. Instead, I met Porter's distrustful gaze. "What he said."

Connor Copper had an amused spark in his eyes as his hand eased away from his weapon.

Porter was still uneasy. "That doesn't explain what either of you are doing here, trespassing on private property."

I wasn't ready to explain my smell-o-vision to the Marseille PD, so I did what any psychic in a similar position would do. I lied. "I took the tour earlier in the day, as you know, and I lost an earring. A diamond one. A gift, even."

"From me," Ezra said, rolling with the tall tale. "I came along to help her find it." He clicked the small light on his keychain. "But then we found something else. We were ready to call you all when the lights came on."

"And why were you hiding behind the door?"

"Just in case you weren't friendly," Ezra told him. "I think we found something connected to your case."

Porter still looked suspiciously at us. "What do you know about my case?"

"Nora filled me in as much as she could," Ezra admitted.

"The point is, Chief Porter, we found something that might be important in solving Darlene's murder."

"And what makes you think she was murdered?"

His question annoyed me. "You mean, other than someone hiding her corpse out in a grape field?"

"Has the medical examiner had a chance to look at her yet?" Ezra asked.

Copper answered. "He did a quick exam about an hour ago."

Porter gave his underling an admonishing glare.

"For heaven's sake," I muttered. "Was there a puncture wound somewhere on her body?"

The set of Porter's mouth went grim, and his jaw flexed. "What did you find?" he ground out.

"Excellent question," I responded with more sarcasm than intended.

"Watch your tone, Ms. Black," Porter cautioned. "My goodwill is about all used up where you're concerned."

I pointed at the floor behind the crates. "A corkscrew over there appears to have dried blood on it." With the lights on, I could see water puddled in various places on the concrete. "The floor is wet. Someone had to have come in here when it was raining out today. They might've stashed the corkscrew in here to hide evidence."

Officer Copper took a quick picture of the corkscrew and its location with his phone before taking a glove from his pocket and putting it on. He picked up the potential weapon and showed it to Chief Porter.

The older man looked upset. "Bag it," he said. "Then

contact the prosecuting attorney's office. I think we have enough for an arrest."

"Who are you arresting?" I asked.

"Not your friend, if that's what you're worried about." He clenched his fists, and his eye twitched. "I think it's time you folks take your party home. You're no longer suspects, and we have your witness statements. If we need anything else from you, someone from our department will be in contact."

"Why are you here?" I asked Porter. "I mean, why this room?"

"An anonymous tip," Officer Copper answered.

"Shut up, Connor!" the chief snapped before turning his anger on us. "Unless you want to be arrested for trespassing and criminal interference in an ongoing case, you'd do well to accept my generous offer to leave my jurisdiction."

"Now wait just a—"

Ezra took my hand. "We'll get out of your hair, Chief," he said. "But I've investigated a fair number of homicides during my career. If you need a hand..."

Porter gave him a look that said, "When Hell freezes over."

Rhonda Nichols walked up behind us. "What are you doing back here? This is private property." Then she saw Chief Porter. "Terry?" Her expression was confused. "What... Is there something you need?"

His sigh almost sounded like a growl as he looked at

the woman and announced, "Rhonda Nichols, I'm placing you under arrest."

You could've flattened me with a board. I had not seen this coming. Of course, my specialty was the past.

The chief retrieved his handcuffs from their pouch on his utility belt and continued, "You have the right to remain silent. If you give up that right, anything you say can and will be held against you in a court of law. Do you understand your rights as I have told them to you?"

"Terry? I don't understand," she said as she allowed herself to be cuffed from behind. "You know me. You know I couldn't do this." She saw the corkscrew as Copper dropped it into a clear evidence bag. "Wait? That's the vintage corkscrew that Tommy gave me on our wedding day. Where did you find that? It went missing a couple of days ago."

"It was right where you dropped it," Porter told her.

I hadn't considered Rhonda an actual suspect. Maybe she *had* faked the will, and Darlene confronted her about it, and she reacted without thinking. None of this seemed premeditated.

Rhonda's eyes were pleading as she passed by me. "I didn't do this," she said again.

"That's what every person I've ever arrested has said," Porter told her. "I want to believe you, but feelings aren't facts. Evidence is."

Porter's cologne was a mixture of wood and spice, and as the aroma hit my nose, the room faded.

"Leave your husband," a man says. His voice is recogniz-

THE VAPES OF WRATH

able as Porter's. He's in a large bed, naked except for a sheet across his lap. A red-haired woman saunters across the room and climbs onto the bed with him. She's also naked, her soft curves swaying as she kisses him.

"I can't," she tells him, and her voice identifies her as Rhonda.

"Why not?"

"Because he's my husband," she says.

"But you're with me." Porter takes her in his arms and cradles her to his chest. "If you love him, why are you here?"

"For joy."

I felt sad for Porter as the memory faded. He cared for Rhonda.

Ezra put his arm around me. "Let's go."

I nodded. I couldn't shake the feeling that this wasn't the end, but as the chief had told Rhonda, feelings weren't facts. There had to be more evidence than just a corkscrew. He wouldn't arrest her on something so circumstantial. It belonged to her. Big deal. Anyone could've taken it and used it, right?

Nope. I pushed the intrusive thoughts from my head.

Not my town, not my people, and not my problem.

So how come I couldn't let it go?

CHAPTER
TWELVE

E zra's truck was in the parking lot, which meant Jordy hadn't left.

"We better let him know it's over," Ezra said.

"Yep. Over."

Ezra grabbed his phone and tapped Jordy's name on his call list. After a second, he frowned. "It went straight to voicemail."

"When we were out in the field earlier, the reception was terrible. Pippa had to run practically back to the winery to get enough of a signal to call the police."

"We should probably go and look for him then."

I led Ezra toward the vineyard. We'd taken a golf cart when Paul had given us the guided tour, but it wasn't a long walk, half a mile at the most. There was a sign posted on the row that doubled as a path to Corked. "This is it."

"I don't see Jordy," Ezra said.

I noticed that the crime scene tape was down, and the police had completely cleared out. "They sure processed the scene fast."

"You said it rained, right?"

"Like God himself was crying."

"Then there probably wasn't much to do once they took pictures of the scene and retrieved her body."

I grunted. "It feels...lazy."

I knew that crime scenes didn't get scoured how they were depicted on television. Most police departments, especially in small towns, had small budgets. Forensics was a money suck. So unless a case was seriously heinous and brutal to crack, there wouldn't be any expensive lab testing or cutting-edge equipment to find a frog's hair on a cricket's butt, as my father said the first time he'd watched an episode of *CSI*. That night, he'd called me out of the blue simply to complain about Hollywood ruining police work.

The ground was mud soup around the base of the vines where we'd discovered Darlene's body. "Gilly tripped on the victim's hand," I told Ezra. "That's how we found her."

His laugh didn't have much humor in it. "Leave it to Gilly to stumble over a dead body."

I couldn't deny his statement. The first time Gilly went out with Scott, she'd tripped into a mobile flambe station and caught herself on fire. Scott scooped her up and jumped into the coy fountain in the middle of the restaurant. Gilly's dress was in tatters, but she only suffered first-degree burns on her legs thanks to Scott's quick thinking. I think that's the moment they both fell in love.

"There's the A-frame," I said, pointing the way. "Jordy must be down there."

"You think it's open?"

"Doubt it. I can't imagine they closed the store and not the bistro." The sun had warmed up the afternoon, and the air was muggy with humidity. "Dang, I'm sweating hard."

"Not yet, but definitely later."

"You're the worst."

"I think you mean the best."

"Correct," I told him with a grin.

He grabbed me at the waist and turned me in his arms. "I love you."

"I love you," I replied. His lips pressed against mine, and I felt the sizzle everywhere. I threaded my hands behind his neck, interlocking my fingers as I raised onto my toes to deepen the kiss. Hot damn, there wasn't a day that had gone by since we started dating that I didn't want him, and he let me know, in no uncertain terms, that he felt the same way.

His hands kneaded my back as he tugged me closer until our bodies were touching. "Whew," he said against my lips. "You require a fire hazard sign."

"Ooops," I giggled. "I left my extinguisher at home."

"Then I guess we'll just have to burn until the flames go out."

I grinned. "I have an endless supply of fuel."

"I'll plan accordingly," he teased. Out of the corner of my eye, I caught movement a few rows over. The vines were tall, and the foliage dense, but it had been something.

Ezra must've felt me stiffen because he asked in a tone that registered high alert, "What's wrong?"

I pressed my forehead to his and spoke softly. "Don't look, but there's movement two rows over at four o'clock."

"You sure?"

"Yes."

Ezra gave me a wink before picking me up and swinging me around. "She said yes!" he shouted.

My fight-or-flight kicked in again, but only for a second. I knew in my heart that he was as interested in getting married as I was, which meant, he wasn't interested at all. We loved what we had, and it didn't matter what anyone else thought we should want.

Ezra set me down on my feet with my back to where I'd seen our watcher and declared, "I have to do this right, baby." He got down on one knee, and my eyes widened. "Nora Black, will you make me the happiest man in the world and..." He stood up, holding a rock in his fist, and I'm not talking about a diamond. This was pure Missouri granite. "...duck," he finished.

I dropped to a squat as Ezra, with a baseball player's speed and accuracy, chucked that rock at the place I'd noted.

A loud yip, followed by a string of cussing, ensued as Connor Copper jumped up from the row and held his side. "That freaking hurt, man!"

"You're lucky it wasn't your head," Ezra told him. "Why are you following us?"

"The chief told me to keep an eye on you and to make sure you leave." He rubbed his ribs. "I'm doing my job."

"You could've stopped us from going into the vineyard," I said. "Why didn't you?"

Copper shuffled his feet and then shrugged. "You're not doing anything illegal."

I stared at him and watched with interest as he avoided my gaze. "What are you really doing, following us?"

"I wasn't lying about the chief," he said. "But...well, I looked you up earlier. You've been a witness in several homicide cases, and you were listed as a police consultant in at least two of them."

I raised my brow. "Okay, so you looked me up. That's not an explanation."

"So, I know someone in Garden Cove that I went to the academy with. I called her." He was toeing the ground nervously now. "She said you're legit."

My stomach flipped. "Legit what?"

"That you see things, and the things you see have helped Detective Holden," he inclined his head to Ezra, "solve murders."

Ezra scowled. "Who did you talk to?"

Copper shook his head. "I won't get her in trouble."

He kind of already did. He'd revealed that the officer was a woman. There were only a dozen on the GCPD, and it wouldn't take much for Ezra to pull their files and find out which one went to the police academy at the same time as Officer Copper.

"Ezra will find out anyhow," I told the younger cop. "He's an excellent detective. You might as well spill."

Copper kept silent. "What do you think happened to Darlene Nichols?"

"You've made an arrest," I said. "You don't need me." I narrowed my gaze at him. "Unless you think you've got the wrong person."

He looked away. Bingo.

Ezra spoke what I was thinking. "You don't think Rhonda Nichols killed her niece."

"I don't," Copper admitted. "And I don't think you do either."

"Your chief isn't going to like you veering off on your own this way," I told him.

"Is it true?" he asked. "Are you a psychic?"

He wasn't messing around. "Sort of," I replied. "I can see memories when they are tied to aromas."

His brow furrowed. "How does that help you find killers?"

I shrugged. "Murder stinks."

Ezra snickered, and I tapped him with my elbow.

He looked at Copper. "Do you want Nora's help?"

"Yes," the cop said. "I want the right person in jail."

119

"We're a packaged deal," Ezra added. "If you get her, you get me as well."

Copper mulled it over for a moment, then nodded. "I can't pay you, and I can't make this official. The chief can't know."

I rolled my eyes. "When you put it like that, I don't know how I can refuse."

"You'll help?"

"I'm saying yes."

Ezra shook his head and smiled. "She's saying yes to all the boys today."

"I have a condition," I bargained.

Copper scratched his head. "Name it."

"Why did you get into a fight with Blake Perkins at Night Owls?"

The young man's mouth dropped open then he closed it. "How did you know about that? It was years ago."

I pointed to Ezra with my chin. "He's a detective. He detected." Technically, it was Shawn who detected it, but it would take too long to explain. "Now, you know a secret about me. I want to know one about you. Blake Perkins. What's the beef?"

"He came out to the Night Owls with a few buddies to start some trouble. I was one of the people he attacked."

"He went there to pick a fight?" Ezra wanted clarification. "Why? What would motivate him to do that?"

"My first guess would be that he's a homophobic dirtbag," Copper said.

"Homophobic?" I uttered.

Copper shook his head. "You should've done more detecting. Night Owls is a gay bar. It's just outside Columbia and the closest one around. Blake and his buddies thought they'd have a good time at our expense."

"And?" Ezra stared at the cop.

Copper stared back. "And I gave him a concussion and broke two of his ribs."

"Good," Ezra said approvingly. "He sounds like he deserved worse."

"Only a few people know about me around here. I'm not ashamed, but I have to be able to do my job without some yahoo thinking I'm an easy target."

"They won't hear about it from us," I said. "And your terms are accepted, but first, we need to find Jordy."

"Who's Jordy?"

"My friend Pippa's husband. He's, uhm, doing some gossip gathering." I glanced around. The area was empty. "Though I'm not sure there's anyone around to gossip with."

As a trio, we marched down the path to Corked. We'd been running from a monsoon when I had been here earlier, so I hadn't appreciated how quaint the place was. It was a rustic A-frame with a deck that wrapped around to the front. The soothing slosh of water lapping onto the shore below the deck added to the romantic charm of the place. I heard voices, and we crossed over the painted deck to go around to the terrace at the back of Corked.

Ezra snorted his amusement when we saw Jordy sitting under an umbrella table, sipping a drink and shooting the breeze with cousin Ellie.

Ezra leaned in close. "I told you. The face of an angel."

CHAPTER

THIRTEEN

J ordy gave us a cordial wave as we piled onto the deck. "Hey, guys," he said. "I was just commiserating with my new friend Ellie here about the joys and woes of running a small business."

"Moo-La-Lattes sounds incredible." Ellie sighed wistfully. "And best of all, no drunks. It makes me want to open a coffee shop." She glanced at Officer Copper as if only now noticing him. "Is something wrong?" She sat up straight. "Did they find who killed Darlene?"

"They've made an arrest," Copper said. "That's all I can say for now. I was just helping these nice folks find their friend."

Ellie nodded. "Thanks so much for earlier," she said to me. "It made me feel better to talk."

"I was glad to lend an ear." I smiled at her. "Is your mother Matilda Carson?"

The blonde tilted her head to the side. "Yes. Do you know her?"

"I had to go to the bank earlier and saw the name outside an office," I lied. "You told me she was an accountant for the bank, so I thought it might be her."

"Oh no." She hopped to her feet. "I didn't tell Mom about Darlene! She probably doesn't know."

"Were they close?"

"Darlene was like my sister," she said. "We shared everything growing up. Even boys, sometimes." Her eyes grew wet with tears. "Momma's going to be so upset." She entered the A-frame and returned seconds later, holding a hobo-style shoulder bag. "I have to go. I'm sorry to leave you all like this. I'm going to lock up, but enjoy the view as much as you want." She smiled at Jordy when he tried to get his wallet out. "You enjoy your Coke. It's on the house." She started to walk away, then turned back one more time. "Thanks for being such a good listener."

Jordy and I both said, "You're welcome."

"Jinx. You owe me a coffee," I informed him.

He smiled. "Deal."

Dang it. Ezra was right. The face of an angel.

* * *

I invited Copper to join us back at the bluff house. He'd told me he had to finish his shift, and I reminded him that following us was on his list of duties.

When we arrived, Gilly and Scott were in the house with Pippa and Tippi.

124

Copper stared at the dry-erase board stuck to the fridge and frowned. "You all have a murder board?

"Yes," I said. "Cool, huh?"

"I've never seen one in person, only on TV."

"We're innovators," Pippa told him. To me, she said, "Nora, why did you bring a police officer to our vacation happy place?"

"Are we in trouble?" Gilly asked. "Or is he the stripper?"

Even with everything going on, I couldn't help but laugh. Gilly for the win. It was her bachelorette, after all. Everyone was smiling. Well, everyone except Tippi.

"You're not here to arrest me, are you?" Tippi inquired. "Because I'll track down someone from last night's meeting to confirm my alibi."

"He wants our help on the case," I answered, putting my hand on her shoulder to calm her. "He knows about my consulting and my aroma-mojo. And no, Gilly, we're not in trouble, and I told you, no stripper. It's not that kind of a bachelorette. And Tippi, they've already arrested someone else."

"Hallelujah!" Gilly pumped her fist into the air, hitting the chandelier above the table. One of the glass crystals fell off and bounced onto the floor. Luckily it didn't break. She blushed as she picked it up. "No breakage, so it doesn't count."

"You're a hot mess," I told my BFF.

"Well, you got the first half right," Scott said as he

put his arms around Gilly. He kissed the side of her neck. "And I can't wait to make you my wife."

"Are you sure?" Gilly teased. "Nora's not wrong about the mess part. You might not realize what you're getting yourself into."

"Gilly," Pippa reproved. She waved her arms in a circle at our bride-to-be-bestie. "Preserve the mystery. It keeps things fresh."

We all laughed.

In the light, I noticed Scott had something shiny clinging to his hair. Gilly had a few sparkles as well.

"Blake's not gay," Copper said. I pivoted to him and saw he was pointing at the murder board. Under Blake's name and at the bottom of his list, it said:

Gay?

Gilly pulled a gold star confetto from Scott's hair and set it on the counter. "Night Owls is a gay bar." She grinned like that cat that ate the mouse. "We got there in time for Glitter-humpday Happy Hour."

I looked askance at Copper.

He shrugged. "It's a Wednesday thing."

"Got it." Honestly, I didn't get it. Once you got glitter-bombed, you were picking glitter for weeks out of places that no glitter should ever go.

"It was fun," Gilly said. "And I finally got to see some half-naked guys for my bachelorette."

Scott groaned with a chuckle. "She told the bartender we were getting married this weekend, and they decided it was something that needed to be celebrated."

"And celebrate, we did," Gilly added. She shook her booty against Scott's leg.

I was beginning to think I'd miscalculated what Gilly wanted for a girls' getaway. "I probably should have flown you to Vegas."

"Uh, no," she said flatly. "Vegas is one of the top ten murder capitals in the United States. It would be like a roach motel. We'd check in, but thanks to your penchant for finding dead bodies, we'd never check out."

"I'm pretty sure you're the one who found the dead body this time."

"Only because you bought the tour tickets."

I opened my mouth to dispute her, then closed it. She wasn't wrong. So instead, I hit her with the all-time conversation-ender ever invented. "Fine."

"I win." She tittered a giggle. "Just saying."

"Whatever." I went over to the murder board. "So, other than Night Owls being a gay bar, any other reason to think Blake is gay, and if he is, does it have any bearing on the case?"

"None of the guys at the bar knew him by name, so maybe not, and no bearing that we could discover." Gilly rolled her hand at me. "Let's go back to the arrest. Who did they pin the murder on?"

"Rhonda Nichols."

"That's a little obvious, don't you think?" Pippa

pointed out. "If she did it, I think she would've acted less, oh, I don't know, guilty."

Tippi steepled her fingers. "She and her daughter were the ones who pointed the finger at me. Classic murderer behavior, sending the cops in the wrong direction. No offense."

Both Copper and Ezra said, "None taken."

"I don't buy it. Rhonda didn't have any motive that I can see."

"Money is a great motivator." Ezra got a soda from the fridge and popped the top. "If Darlene had proof that the will was invalid, that's a least a few million dollars' worth of motive."

I shook my head. "It wasn't just Darlene out in the hall talking about the will not being legal."

"When did this happen?" Copper asked.

"Last night at the bar," I told him. "When Tippi and I were in the restroom, we overheard Darlene and a man talking about Thomas Nichol's will. Darlene was certain the will had been forged. Rhonda would've had to kill more than just one person to keep the secret. Besides, a corkscrew as a weapon and the body being covered haphazardly near the main walking path..."

"Right," Ezra agreed. "It was a disorganized kill. Someone wasn't thinking straight, if they were thinking at all."

"Rhonda strikes me as someone who wouldn't panic."

"This was a murder of opportunity," Scott surmised.

"They've managed to pin it on a viable suspect," Jordy added. "Even if they did it quickly, the plan to frame Rhonda was smart."

"They wouldn't have had much time to do it," Copper chipped in. "The medical examiner put the death between five and eight in the morning."

"That's not very long," I said. "Her skin was cold."

"He said she had been somewhere freezing for at least an hour. Her skin and tissue had cold damage, and rigor had set in, but her internal organs were still warm."

"What's the evidence against Rhonda?" Ezra asked.

"There was a hair in Darlene's hand that matched Rhonda's. On top of that, a witness, one of the field workers who had come in early, put Rhonda at the winery at a quarter to five, and she says she worked until opening at ten a.m., but no one can corroborate because she was in her," he finger-quoted the next words, "office going over invoices."

"And the corkscrew?"

"We got an anonymous tip that someone saw her enter the fermentation room holding a bloody weapon and that she came out without it, around ten-thirty."

"What was she wearing?" I asked.

"I don't know," Copper replied. "Why?"

"Because I saw the killer throw the corkscrew behind the crate, and they were in a rain suit. One similar to what Chief Porter wore when he got to the scene after the storm."

129

Copper shook his head emphatically. "Even if the chief were guilty, he'd never set up Rhonda. The arrest nearly broke him."

"I'm not saying it was him. The suit fit the person as if made for someone much bigger." I chewed the inside of my lower lip for a moment. "It rained around nine this morning but then didn't rain again until after noon. The person I saw was wet. They left water puddled on the floor of the fermentation room, so they were either there between nine and nine-thirty, or they were there when the rain came down at noon."

"Hold on." Copper took out his phone and texted someone. A few seconds later, his phone buzzed. He read the message and said, "Her prints were on the weapon. As far as the prosecutor is concerned, that seals the deal."

"No." I shook my head. "The person who dumped the weapon was wearing gloves. Why would Rhonda do that if she wasn't going to wipe down the handle?"

Gilly sighed. "They definitely have the wrong person."

I concurred. "Yep, they have the wrong person."

Ezra leaned back in his chair and rubbed his jawline with his knuckles. "Do you know if they found anything else on Darlene that could be considered suspicious or around where she was hidden?"

"There was a puncture wound at the base of her skull. It's what killed her. Death wasn't instantaneous, according to the doctor. There was a large contusion on the back of her head, evidence of choking, and the corkscrew had been screwed into the top of her spine, severing the cord from her brain."

Pippa looked ill. "That's awful. I'm going to be sick." She fled the room with Jordy trailing behind.

Tippi looked worried. "She's been sick a lot lately," the younger Davenport confessed. "She doesn't think it's bad enough to see her doctor."

I made a note to force Pippa to go to the doctor after we got back to Garden Cove.

"Scott can look Pippa over, right?" Gilly's brown eyes were hopeful as she stared at her fiancé.

"Of course," he said. "I'm happy to get the ball rolling."

That seemed to mollify both Tippi and Gilly. Admittedly, it made me feel a little better as well. Pippa had not been herself lately. She'd been cranky, worried about every little thing, and short-tempered. I'd written it off as a phase, but now I was worried it went deeper than a reaction to increased stress and anxiety.

Copper's phone buzzed again. He read the message and then said, "How do you all feel about sticking around for one more day?"

"As long as we're out of here on Friday," Gilly warned the rest of us.

"What she said," I told Copper.

"Good, because tomorrow night at seven, the family of Darlene Nichols is holding a vigil at La Sous Terre, and they are inviting anyone who wants to pay their respects."

"All the suspects in one place," Ezra mused. "I like it."

I wasn't sure I liked it, but it had the glorious smack of convenience. "We'll be there," I told him.

And maybe if I got really lucky, I could sniff out the killer and stop him or her from getting away with murder.

CHAPTER

FOURTEEN

The next day we stopped all investigations directly to enjoy a long stroll by the river. We'd packed sandwiches and drinks the men carried in backpacks we bought from Dollar General. Pippa was right. For a small store, it had a fantastic assortment of goods.

The sun's reflection made the water's surface a shiny mirror that reflected every nearby tree, cliff, and cloud.

"It is beautiful here." Gilly reclined onto a large red and white polka-dotted picnic blanket and gazed out over the water. "That is, if you can avoid the dead bodies."

We laughed, but not because we were callous about Darlene's death. It came down to the old adage that if we don't laugh, we'll cry. Darlene had been someone's daughter, sister, lover, and friend. Regardless of how she'd behaved toward Tippi, she didn't deserve to have her young life taken from her. The cruel tenacity of the killer to crank a corkscrew through flesh and bone was beyond depraved. I knew with one hundred percent certainty that no matter how much we joked, we never lost sight of the fact that someone lost their life.

I leaned back against Ezra as he put his arms around me. "What are you thinking about?" he asked.

"Darlene," I said. "I hope we can give her the justice she deserves."

Pippa rolled to her side on the picnic blanket. "I think she'd be okay with Rhonda going to jail. Darlene struck me as the vengeful type."

"Who gets the business now?" Tippi asked, perplexed. "If Rhonda goes to jail, will she still own the place? Will it go to Paul as the last owner's blood relative? Or will her daughter Donna get everything?"

Pippa sat up. "If Thomas Nichols died three months ago, chances are good that his will is still in probate, which means it hasn't been executed yet. However, unless there's some kind of morals clause, she can still inherit even if she goes to jail."

Tippi mulled over the information momentarily, then asked, "Why frame her, then? I mean, if she gets the money regardless, what's the point?"

"Excellent question, Tip," I said.

"Maybe it gets her out of the way," Scott remarked.

"Maybe it gets her out of the way," I repeated. "What if that's the exact right answer?"

Gilly put her hand on mine. "If we don't catch the

bad guy tonight, we're still leaving in the morning, right?"

"Absolutely," I promised. "Wedding trumps everything."

She exhaled a held breath. "Thank you."

I didn't tell her that I would come back after the wedding was over. I was too invested in this case to leave it up to fate. Besides, if it were one of us in jail for something we didn't do, I'd hope someone would fight for us. Our first case was similar. Gilly had been arrested because of circumstantial evidence. Her knife had been found in the body of her ex-boyfriend. If I hadn't used my gift, who knows what might've happened?

Pippa stretched. "Naps before vigil?"

"Oh, hell yes," Gilly rejoiced. "That's my vote."

"Mine too," I seconded.

Ezra, Scott, and Jordy were in agreeance. Tippi was the only holdout. "I'll go back to the house with you all, but I refuse to nap."

I hung back with her while we walked. "Tell me what's going on with Pippa? How long has she been sick?" My friend's illness had weighed on me the night before. It's one of the many reasons I'd slept terribly and needed a nap.

"She started sleeping all the time about a month ago. I swear, if she's not at work or taking care of J.J., she's sacked out. She slept twelve hours last Saturday. She never sleeps that long. On top of that, she's been paranoid and emotional. I swear, Nora, I can't lose her. She's the only family that matters to me."

"We're not going to lose her," I said. "I'll make sure she sees a doctor next week." Scott gave her a once-over at the bluff house and said she'd need labs to figure out why she was feeling fatigued and experiencing mood swings. He also said her symptoms could be something as simple as anemia or a vitamin deficiency, or even perimenopause. I hoped it was something simple and survivable. I couldn't help but think about how the cancer had taken so much from my mother before it finally just took her. I prayed that I wouldn't have to lose someone else I loved to the awful disease.

Tippi's shoulders eased. "Thank you. I've been afraid to say anything, so thank you for asking."

"Pippa's my sister too." I put my arm over her shoulder. "And you have more family than just her." I pointed at our lovely group of friends. "You have all of us."

Tears shone in Tippi's eyes. "Thanks. I feel the same way." Her gaze held a longing as she watched Jordy and Pippa walk hand in hand. "You think I'll ever get a happily ever after?"

I snorted a laugh. "You know those don't exist, right?"

Why were people so obsessed with happily ever after? I married my first husband with the idea that we would be together forever, and the relationship ended before my twenty-fifth birthday. The first few years of our marriage were wonderful, and while the ending was sad, I wouldn't have given up the good to avoid the bad.

"I think I'd rather be alone than get my heart broken," she said.

"Bah," I scoffed. "This idea that being alone is better than getting your heart broken doesn't leave much room for joy and happiness." I smiled as I watched Ezra's cute butt as he walked next to Scott and Gilly. I gave Tippi a nudge to look ahead. "Even if Ezra and I ended tomorrow, I'd be so extremely grateful for our time together. I'm happy for now, every single day I'm with him. I have zero regrets. Stop worrying about getting your heart broken. It's a resilient muscle built to take a few punches and return stronger than before." I squeezed my young friend before removing my arm from her. "Time has a way of healing wounds. As they say, no risk, no reward."

"Is this your way of telling me to go big or go home?"

I laughed. "You don't have to do either. I know you've done a lot of things that have hurt you in the past. You're working the program. One day at a time and all that. What does your sponsor say?"

"She says I've been sober long enough that I can and should start taking the next steps in my future." Tippi looked down at the sidewalk and brushed her hair back from her face. "I can barely take care of myself. I can't take care of someone else."

My loud bark of disbelief had all our friends glancing back over their shoulders. "We're fine," I told them, waving them to keep going.

Tippi looked chagrinned. "You think I'm not ready, too?"

"I think you've been taking care of someone else—and doing it brilliantly, I might add—for over two years now. J.J. is thriving. You have taking care of someone else down to a science." I slowed my pace for a moment and looked her in the eye. "Honestly, you don't need someone else to make you happy." I gave her chest a light tap. "The happiness has to start here. If you're ready to date, then date. Kiss a lot of toads in the process." I grinned as Scott goosed Gilly, and she let out a peal of delight. "Gilly sure did. If you don't feel ready, that's okay too. Just stop living scared to make a decision and find a way to love yourself, warts and all. It will make you much happier than chasing something you're not sure you even want. Happiness attracts happiness, and love will come when it comes."

Tippi took my words in for several silent steps. Finally, she nodded. "Dang, Nora, you're like a guru."

"I'm just someone who was never very good at settling for the things she didn't want. Don't settle, Tip. Life's too short." I picked up my walking pace. "You good?"

She nodded. "Better. Thanks, Nora."

With sincerity, I said, "That's what family's for."

I DIDN'T END up napping. Instead, I stared at the freaking murder board for two hours. Copper had given us additional information.

None of the family members had solid alibis, which meant any of them could've been the killer. Paul said he'd arrived at the winery at eight-thirty and had gone to the barrel room to test the aging wine for spoilage and bacteria. He'd told the police that he hadn't left the area until right before eleven, when Rhonda told him he was giving the wine tour.

Ellie said she'd been home until nine and then went to Corked to start prepping all the ingredients for the sandwiches she sells. The first customers arrived at eleven-fifteen. Donna said she'd been home all morning and only arrived at eleven, when she saw Paul with a group of women in the shop, getting ready to take the tour. That was Pippa, Gilly, Tippi, and me.

I was inclined to take Ellie off the list because I'd seen someone throw the corkscrew behind those boxes during the storm. Ellie had been in the cellar at the time. We were her alibi.

Blake said he got wasted the night before and had passed out on his couch. He was awakened by the storm. That's when he called one of his buddies, who told him to come to the vineyard because of an accident.

Chief Porter, our least likely suspect, had gone to work at five in the morning. Copper said there was video evidence at the precinct of the chief leaving the station at nine forty-five. He also said the chief had admitted to meeting up with Rhonda shortly after at ten-fifteen. They spent a little over an hour together having sex in Rhonda's office before getting into a disagreement with her about their relationship. He left the winery shortly after. That must've been when he passed us in the parking lot.

"Shower's open," Ezra said, patting his hair dry with a towel. "See anything new?"

"Not a damn thing," I responded. "But the night is young."

He wore jeans and a light aqua-blue t-shirt. "I didn't bring anything fancy," he said. "Is this good enough?"

"Always." I kissed him. "The clothes are good too."

"We'll get this figured out," he assured me. "One way or the other."

"I know." I ran my fingers through his damp hair. "One way or another."

CHAPTER
FIFTEEN

The vigil started at seven, and we pulled into the parking lot of La Sous Terre ten minutes before the event. I didn't want to chance that some of the suspects would leave before we got there. The lot was wall-to-wall with cars and trucks, and we'd had to park on the street. A crowd had formed on the front patio, eagerly waiting for the doors to open. I didn't know if it was neighborly or ghoulish that so many folks had come out to pay their respects.

Murmured words of sympathy, along with tears and laughter, grew louder as we made our way into the mix.

"We went to school together," I heard one woman say. "She was always so nice."

"Such a pretty girl," an older woman told the man next to her. "Too young."

"Let's leave by eight-thirty," a guy said. "There's a new episode of *Survival Games* on tonight."

"It'll be on the DVR," the lady next to him chided. "You can watch it later."

"Later, I'll be sleeping. Some of us still have work in the morning."

So far, the vigil reminded me of my dad's funeral. He'd been a public figure, and when he passed, a lot of the town came out to pay their respects. It was a mix of those who loved him, those who knew him, those whom he'd served, and the bored people who were looking for an interesting way to kill time.

We were in the "none of the above" category. I wouldn't feel easy until Darlene's real killer was behind bars. Unless... I turned to Ezra. "Maybe the murderer was someone who was just passing through."

His eyes were soft. "No," he replied. "Whoever did this set Rhonda up to take the fall. It wasn't any stranger."

"I knew it was a shot in the dark."

Statistically, most murder victims knew their killers. A Department of Justice study found that sixteen percent of the time, in all cases, the defendant was a family member, and sixty-four percent of the time, it was a friend or acquaintance. Those numbers put a real crimp in all the "stranger danger" our parents taught us when we were young, especially since the danger was often closer to home. Even so, I hated the idea that someone Darlene was supposed to trust was responsible for her death.

I spotted Copper standing near Chief Porter. He was

risking his job by asking us to stay and help right this wrong. So, when his gaze met mine briefly before he looked away, I didn't take it personally. We all had a part to play.

Gilly dangled her forearms on top of Ezra's and my shoulders. "What's the plan, Stan?"

"Oh, you know. Look around, smell things, try not to get beat up."

Gilly did *not* laugh. "The last part for sure, babes."

Paul, looking solemn, opened the front door. Ellie stood beside him on one side, and an older woman, whom Ellie resembled, took the position on his other side. I assumed it was Matilda Carson. The crowd grew quiet, waiting to hear what he had to say.

Paul clasped his hands in front of him. "Thank you all for coming out tonight. We can feel your thoughts and prayers, and they bring us so much comfort."

Ellie began to cry, and Matilda reached across the front of Paul to hand her daughter a tissue. There were a few tearful sniffs from the onlookers.

Paul gave his cousin and aunt sympathetic nods. "My grandfather started this business almost ninety years ago. His son took over when he died, and my uncle after that. My sister and I discovered that Rhonda Nichols coerced my uncle to leave her the *family* land and business." He shook his head. "My sister recently found proof of this, and Rhonda killed her for it. The proof has gone suspiciously missing since my sister's death, but I know you all will support us in taking back what's ours."

You could've scraped my jaw off the parking lot. Was Paul using the vigil as a power play to take Rivière Tranquille back from Rhonda?

Yes, he was.

"Wow," Gilly muttered. "His sister's not even cold and dead yet. This is morbid."

I nodded. "It's a little gross."

"People can have strange reactions to grief," Jordy said. He and Pippa had moved up closer behind us. "A guy I worked with in construction lost his wife to an overdose while he slept next to her. He called the cops when he woke up and realized she was gone, and after her body was removed in the middle of the night, he went to work the next day like nothing had happened. Not a single person on the job, including me, knew she was dead for weeks. He clocked in, joked around, ate lunch with everyone, and for all intents and purposes, he acted his normal self." Jordy closed his eyes at the memory. "Then, one day, we found him sobbing in the maintenance truck and trying to drink bleach. He said he couldn't live without her."

"Yikes," Scott muttered, but he nodded his head. "In the emergency room, I see a lot of crazy reactions when someone loses a loved one, from denial to anger to a full-on collapse. I even had one woman who started laughing and couldn't stop. Her oxygen levels got seriously low, so we had to sedate her to prevent hypoxia."

"All right," I said. They'd made their point. I'd give Paul the benefit of the doubt, but this show he was putting on rubbed me the wrong way.

"I want to give my sincerest thanks to Chief Porter for the expediency in which he investigated my sister's case." Paul bowed his head. "This tragedy has brought home how important family is." He held out his hands for his cousin and aunt. The two women slipped their palms in his. The show of solidarity was a nice gesture. Still, it gave me the ick. "Once the murderer has been brought to justice, and we have our heritage returned, we pledge to devote land and resources to boost the economy in Marseille."

The assembled mass clapped and cheered. I spotted Blake and Donna standing near each other at the front of the group. They were several feet apart, so I didn't think they were together.

"Lock her up!" someone shouted. "Throw away the key!"

"For Darlene," another person yelled. Then the chant went up, and there was a chorus of, "Lock her up! Throw away the key! For Darlene!"

Blake looked glassy-eyed, like he'd been drinking for a week. Donna looked pissed, and the more they chanted, the redder her face got until she stormed off and out of my line of sight.

Chief Porter nervously scanned the throng. Copper had his hand on his taser. The chief, several times, talked into the radio clipped onto a shoulder strap. Probably telling the rest of his people to stay alert.

I didn't blame him. "This isn't a vigil," I told Ezra. "It's a rally."

"Vigilante is only one letter away from vigilant," Scott said.

"He sure is getting everyone riled up." Gilly looked less enthusiastic. "This might've been a bad idea."

The mourners continued to chant. Paul and his cousin Ellie joined in. Matilda didn't. She stood there numbly, looking dumbstruck and exhausted.

"Sometimes people just need an excuse to act stupid." Ezra shrugged. "Mob mentality is a real thing. If one person says the wrong thing, this could get ugly fast."

"We need to stay out of the middle." Jordy took Pippa's hand and started dragging her to the left where the crowd was thinner.

The rest of us, as a group, followed them out.

Copper left his post next to the chief and met us at the edge.

"Porter wants to know why you haven't left town," Copper informed us. "I told him that the house you're renting was non-refundable and you'd demanded to get your money's worth."

"Ah, the callous tourist ploy. Works every time." I knew from living in a resort town that some people, when they were on vacation, felt as if the locals owed them a good time. "Did that mollify him?"

Copper nodded. "I'm supposed to be strongly suggesting you all take yourselves somewhere other than here." He had his hand closed in a fist and when he turned it over, he produced a silver key. His gaze pivoted toward La Sous Terre. "It's the key to the delivery door on the south side. Paul Nichols gave it to me earlier when I searched Rhonda's office at the restaurant. I'll return it tomorrow."

Without a GPS, my sense of direction was crap. I was going to require landmarks. I closed my fingers around the key and asked, "Left side, right side, or back?"

Copper smirked, his voice was a soft growl as he spoke through barely moving lips. "Left side. There is an alcove that will keep you hidden, but it's not very big. You can't go in all at once. It would be too conspicuous. Paul is planning a candle lighting as soon as the sun sets. That will be your time to go." He glanced over his shoulder at the chief. "I better get back before he gets suspicious."

"Let's go back to the vehicles," I suggested. "When it gets dark, we'll go in."

"Good call," Ezra agreed.

* * *

I hoped our leaving the area mollified Porter. Copper had asked for our help, and I didn't want to make trouble for the young cop. He was bright. I liked that in my police officers. I worried that Porter might accuse us of trying to interfere in an investigation, but Ezra reminded me that he'd made an arrest. The investigating part was over as far as the chief was concerned.

I'd seen the pain in his expression when he'd put the cuffs on Rhonda, and the vision had pre-confirmed what Copper said about the chief caring for the widow.

When the sun finally set, Ezra said, "Ready to go?"

A tap at Ezra's truck window made me *yeep*. It was Gilly. She'd been in my car with Scott, Pippa, Jordy, and Tippi. I glared at her for scaring me.

Ezra rolled down the window.

"You about made me pee my pants," I accused.

"It's dark," she said, without defense. "The candles are being lit."

I eyed her with suspicion. "I've had Lasik, so I can see that."

"I have to pee," Gilly finally announced. "I'm going with you."

Pippa popped up behind her. "Me too."

Scott, Jordy, and Tippi were stationed behind them. "Do you all have to pee, too?" I asked.

"No." Scott shook his head. "But Gilly's not going in there without me."

"Same for Pippa," Jordy said.

My gaze dropped on Tippi. She shrugged. "I'm not staying alone in the car. It's dark and there's a murderer on the loose."

"Fair point." I looked at Ezra. "Copper said to keep the party small."

He looked at our pals. "I think this is as small as we're getting."

"Stealth," I cautioned. "Be like the shadows." I stared at Gilly pointedly. "Try not to trip, catch on fire, or break anything."

She crossed her arms over her ample chest. "Do I have to remind you this is my bachelorette getaway?"

"No." I sounded as surly as I felt. "Fine. Go light something on fire."

Gilly's expression was smug. "I might just do that."

She was kidding. At least, I hoped.

"We can't all approach from the same direction," Ezra said. "Jordy and Pippa, go around the back on the right. Scott and Gilly, take a forward approach, then come around the front to the left side. We'll leave the door blocked open, make sure you all get there at different times, so you don't draw attention to yourselves."

"What about me?" Tippi asked.

"You go with Pippa and Jordy."

"And I suppose you two are taking the direct route," Pippa said.

I smiled at her. "I have the key."

CHAPTER
SIXTEEN

Ten minutes later, Ezra and I had woven, unseen, past two uniformed officers and dozens of folks holding candles while singing "Candle in the Wind" by Elton John. It seemed a little on the nose for my taste, but at least they weren't shouting about throwing away the key anymore.

The alcove on the side of the building was arched and lined with the same stone and stucco brick that made up the rest of the restaurant's exterior. It was recessed three feet deep and had a metal security door nestled inside. I took the key from my pocket. Ezra used the mini flashlight on the keyhole so I could see what I was doing. Very helpful. The lock was stiff, but after a quick jiggle, the key slid in. I turned it to the left and felt the click as the door opened.

"We're in," I said. The moment I took the key out, the tumbler clicked again. It was the kind of door that locked every time it was closed. There was a loose brick on the ground near the wall of the alcove. Probably used to prop the door open when they were carrying in supplies. "Use that to keep it open."

Ezra placed the brick between the doorjamb and the threshold to act as a wedge. "That'll do it." He held the door open until I was inside then gently closed it after us, making certain not to dislodge the foothold. "Careful." His voice was hushed. Reverent, like the kind of tone you used in a church or library.

The small hall connected to the door went directly into the kitchen. I could hear a faint murmur coming from outside the restaurant of raised voices in song. I recognized the new melody as "Dust in the Wind" by Kansas. It was a bit corny considering the circumstances, but I couldn't fault their taste. I had the song on every mixtape I'd ever made in high school.

Ezra and I made our way through the industrial, professional kitchen. It had been thoroughly cleaned. The scent of bleach and lemon was prevalent. Gilly's ex-husband Gino had kept a tip-top kitchen, but this one was beyond sanitized. I brushed against something wet and saw it was a washcloth, still damp with water. The cleaning had to have been done today sometime. I decided it was probably not important. The chef might've been taking advantage of an unscheduled down day.

"No, no," a voice, high-pitched with stress, whines. A woman, I'm guessing because of the voice, is wearing a

biohazard suit covering her from head to toe, and an N-95 mask like they use in hospitals. "There's so much gross blood."

Is this where Darlene was killed? Was I seeing her murderer cleaning up evidence?

No. It's not that. She's holding a plastic sack that's full of a dark red substance. It sloshes around, making a wet sucking sound every time she moves it. The stench is overpowering, like that of rancid chicken and beef. "Too much blood and it's putrid. I think the smell is clinging to my skin. What are we going to do?"

A voice, crackling as if coming through a cellphone with a bad connection, says, "Do what you can to get as much mixed into the hamburger so as not to be detected. I have faith in you, darling."

"This wasn't part of the deal," the woman cries. There is a tinkling sound I hear over the static, and it's oddly familiar. The woman in the cellar making out with Paul? Possibly. "I didn't agree to this," she complains. "I want our plan to work, but not by giving everyone food poisoning."

"How did ... think this ... going to ... down ... dawn...? Don't ... such ... Daft," the voice says as the phone begins cutting in and out.

She lets out a shriek of frustration then reaches over and taps the call closed. Leaving the bag on the counter, she goes to a nearby cabinet and retrieves a can of lemon-scented antimicrobial spray and liberally sprays the air.

"What did you see?" Ezra asked the second I came out of the memory.

"Someone trying to taint the food of the restaurant." I went into detail about the bag of rotten meat, the smell, the weird conversation. "I'm pretty sure whoever the two of them are, they were trying to ruin the restaurant."

"Why?"

"Revenge?" I shook my head. "The woman was in full hazmat, and the guy was talking over a cellphone with lousy reception."

"It's never easy," Ezra said, running his hands through his hair in frustration.

"Nope. It never is."

"Hey," Gilly said from behind me.

I jumped. "Don't sneak up on people."

"You said stealth," Gilly told me. "Where's the bathroom?"

I pointed at the swinging kitchen door. "Out there somewhere."

"Where dreams come true?" Gilly asked.

I couldn't help it. I laughed. My BFF was a song nerd. "If your dream is to pee, then yes."

Scott had moved to stand next to Ezra. His gaze darted around the room and he looked extremely nervous. "Did you get anything yet?"

Wow. He wasn't nervous, he was excited. Gilly's fiancé liked to live on the edge. I smiled at him. He fit right in with our ragtag bunch.

"Spoiled meat and bad reception."

He managed to look only mildly disappointed. "What can I do to help?"

I'd been playing with my gift back in Garden Cove. Trying to see memories specific to the scents that I chose. Sometimes it worked. "Can you guys fan out and start smelling everything? Go to the bar area, the bandstand, the restaurant, storage closets, whatever you can find. If you find any aroma that stands out, come and get me. It'll be easier than me trying to sniff everything by myself."

Scott's shoulders straightened. "You got it."

"Heard," Pippa said as she came into the kitchen with Jordy and Tippi. "We'll get started on the sniff-a-palooza."

The four of them departed, leaving Ezra and me alone. "I'm clueless right now."

"That's why we're here," he encouraged. "To get a clue." Ezra and I continued to search the kitchen, the pantry, and even the refrigerator and freezer. Copper had said that Darlene had been flash frozen on the outside, but not long enough to get her insides cold. I had flashes of memories that involved mostly work, and one guy who masturbated into a napkin while naked in the freezer. Ick. I might never eat out again. Regrettably, none of the memories helped me to figure out Darlene's murder.

Pippa poked her head in the door. "Nora, we got something for you."

I followed her to the bar where Scott had put a

container of cherries, cut limes and lemons, and pineapple wedges on the polished bar. "These fruits smell super fruity."

"As they do." I smiled.

Tippi set a can of leather polish and a used chamois next to them. "This definitely stinks."

Jordy one-upped them with a bottle of perfume. "Found it in the office," he said.

"Excellent work, team." I looked around. "Where's Gilly?"

Pippa frowned. "I haven't seen her."

"Didn't you go to the bathroom? That's where she was headed when she came in."

"I was just in there." Pippa sounded as alarmed as I felt. "She wasn't in there."

Scott rushed around the bar. "Where are the bathrooms?"

Pippa pointed at a narrow hall on the right side of the bandstand. "That way."

I was hot on Scott's tracks as he ran to the hall, throwing open doors. Men's toilet, janitor closet, and women's toilet. Gilly wasn't in any of them.

"Where is she?" Panic had replaced excitement. "We have to find her."

We started opening every door we could find, and I fought down my worst fears. Every time I'd disappeared on a case, it was usually because some bad guy was trying to kill me. "Gilly!" I yelled, not giving a flying fig if anyone outside the restaurant might hear.

The others joined me. By the fourth time I yelled for Gilly, she popped her head out of a door on the opposite side of the restaurant from the bathrooms. "I'm here!"

I wanted to freaking throttle her. "What in the ever-loving world are you doing? You scared the crap out of me." I gestured to our relieved friends and her panicked fiancé. "I thought Scott was going to have a heart attack."

"I'm sorry." She held her hands up in surrender. "But I think you'll want to check this out." She pointed to the door she'd exited. "There's a wine cellar down here, and it looks like there might've been a scuffle. I found some broken glass on the floor."

I exhaled a noisy, exasperated sigh as I marched past her.

"Sorry," she said with a wince. "I didn't realize I'd been gone for very long. You know how I get around wine."

Scott wrapped her in his arms and held her so tight I thought she might break. I heard him say, "Don't you disappear on me ever again. I don't know what I'd do if anything happened to you."

"I won't," she promised. "Not ever again."

Ezra joined me at the top of the cellar stairs. "I'm going with you."

"I'm good with that." I still felt shaky from worry and was glad for Ezra's steadying hand. "I hope this leads somewhere because I'm not sure I can take much more."

"We can leave right now if you want. I'll pack your bags myself. We can be in Garden Cove in time to sleep in your bed." He waved a hand. "No judgment at all."

It was a tempting offer. Especially sleeping in my own bed. My sense of right and wrong was going to put me six feet under one of these days, but it drove me. "You know I can't."

He grinned sheepishly. "I know."

The cellar was cool and damp. There was a wine chiller full of white wines, and the walls were lined with wooden crisscrossed wine racks, with bottles stacked in each opening.

"The broken glass is on the right side," Gilly yelled down. "And the wood on the rack there is freshly chipped and splintered. I noticed the glass first."

I walked over and squatted next to the chip. "I see it!" I shouted up to her. But I didn't see the glass yet. I got on my knees and put my eyes closer to the floor. There was a faint whiff of wine and something else. A cologne or perfume, maybe. It had raspberry notes that mixed with the earthiness of the wine.

I inhaled the aroma deeply, trying to decipher every base, then...

"Help," a woman says as she pulls herself along the floor. There is blood matting the blonde hair on the back of her head and she has her left hand closed into a tight fist. "God, help me," she cries. A wine bottle with dark green glass is shattered on the floor, and the back of her shirt is wet with the spirits. She drops something on the ground in front of the

rack, then uses her fingertips to flick it under the wood. She scratched at the base of the x, picking at the wood until it chips and her nail breaks.

A door slams open, and heavy footsteps echo off the cellar walls as someone runs down the stairs. The person is dressed in gray rain gear that fits loose. It's the same person who had disposed of the corkscrew. They hold the corkscrew in their right hand and stalk toward Darlene.

I gasped as the vision ended. There was so much fear and horror tied up in Darlene's memory that it made me sick to my stomach.

"Hand me your light," I said.

Ezra obliged. With penlight in hand, I got low to the floor and peered under the base of the rack. That's when I saw what Darlene had so valiantly hidden as her way of pointing the finger at her killer—and everything became crystal clear.

As I rose to my feet, I met Ezra's gaze. "I know who killed Darlene."

CHAPTER
SEVENTEEN

I left the object where I found it. It was evidence, and moving it was tantamount to tampering. "We have to get Copper," Ezra said. "He'll need to take steps to reopen the investigation."

I still felt ill from the vision. The cruelty and lack of humanity it took to kill Darlene so viciously was like a horror movie.

Ezra and I walked back up the stairs slowly. My legs felt as if I had two large sandbags attached, but I was too proud to ask him to carry me. When we exited, none of our friends were in the hall.

"Gilly?" I called out. "Pippa? Tippi!"

"In here," a man replied. "Come join us."

Ezra's mouth thinned as his frown deepened.

"Chief Porter," I greeted him as we walked into the bar area. Pippa, Jordy, Tippi, Scott, and Gilly sat on barstools, looking like elementary students waiting to be called in by the principal. Copper stood to the left of Porter. He had his hands crossed in front of his body, and his head down. In a strange way, his presence was a source of comfort. He was rational, smart, and he would fight the chief to keep us out of trouble.

It's what I chose to believe.

"Ms. Black, didn't I tell you to get out of town?"

"You don't own this town, Chief Porter, so I'm not sure you get to kick me out." I put up a hand to stop his retort. "Besides, I think you're going to want to hear what I know."

"How can you know anything? Dating a police officer doesn't make you a cop." He scowled.

"He's a detective," I corrected. "And my skills have nothing to do with who I date. I've been around police work my entire life, and it doesn't take a genius to figure out that you arrested the wrong person for Darlene Nichols' murder."

He blustered, "Now, you wait just a damn minute."

Gilly, who is usually pleasant and nice to a fault, snapped, "No, *you* wait just a damn minute. Nora has been working double time to find the real killer while you've been, what? Arresting the wrong person and babysitting a bunch of jackholes who would love to see her locked up for life? What happened to presumed innocent until proven guilty?"

"Unless you have a better suspect, you need to watch your mouth, missy," Porter said menacingly.

Scott put his arm around Gilly and glared at Porter as if to say, "I double dog dare you."

"I know who killed Darlene," I said bluntly. "And I can prove it."

"How?" Porter asked.

He hadn't tried to play off my declaration as moronic, which told me that he was interested in learning what I had to say.

I didn't sugarcoat the truth. He'd either believe me or he wouldn't. "I'm psychic. I see other people's memories."

"Bah!" He swatted the air with the back of his hand. "I'm about two seconds away from arresting you, Ms. Black. You need to tell the truth."

"I am." I walked over and got close enough to smell him again. Only, I didn't need to. "You've been having an affair with Rhonda Nichols since before her husband died."

He scoffed at me.

I stood my ground. "You asked her to leave her husband, and she told you no because she was married. Then you asked her why she was with you, and she told you, for joy."

Porter blanched and grabbed the back of a chair for purchase. "Every time," he murmured. "She said it every time."

Good, he was finally listening to me. "I think I can get a confession," I told him, "but first, I'm going to need all the suspects together."

Porter crossed his arms. "I don't care what kind of psychic mumbo-jumbo you think you got going on, this isn't some mystery show where you get to rattle off a bunch of nonsense until the guilty party confesses."

Ezra put his arm around my shoulder. "It is, if that's what Nora wants."

Out of the side of my mouth, I told my sweetie, "What I really want is my murder board." Not because it had any revelatory secrets. I just thought it would freak them the hell out.

Porter glanced over at Copper. "What do you think?"

"I think we should take Ms. Black and Detective Holden seriously and give them what they want."

Porter looked uncertain, but he said, "Who do I need to grab?"

"They're all here," I said. "Except Rhonda. I need Donna Patterson, Paul Nichols, Ellie Nichols, Blake Perkins, and Rhonda Nichols if you can manage it."

"I'm the chief," he stated flatly. "I can manage. Give me an hour, and I'll have everyone..."

"Here," I said. "It has to be here, where the murder took place."

"Okay, Ms. Black. You got one shot. If you make me look like a fool, Rhonda will have some company behind bars tonight."

"The only one looking like a fool will be the killer."

PIPPA, Gilly, Scott, and Jordy set up a circle of chairs. Ezra had gone back to the bluff house and retrieved the murder board. For the sake of peace amongst the ranks, he had removed Chief Porter's name from the list.

The chief, along with Copper and five other officers, escorted Ellie, Donna, Paul, Blake, and Rhonda into the restaurant. Ellie looked bewildered, Rhonda defeated, Donna still pissed, and Paul confused. Blake, on the other hand, looked like he was about to pass out. I could smell the bourbon on him from across the room.

"Why are we here?" Paul demanded. "And why are these people trespassing on our private property?"

His outrage sparked something in Rhonda. "It's *my* private property, Paul. Not yours. And they have my permission to burn the place to the ground if they want to."

His eyes bugged, and he swallowed back whatever retort was on the tip of his tongue.

"No worries. I have no interest in burning the building to the ground," I said. But that didn't mean I wouldn't be starting fires.

Once everyone was seated, I nodded to Ezra. On cue, he brought the murder board into the circle and put it on one of the chairs.

"What in the hell is that?" Donna shook her fist. She had a charm bracelet that tinkled when in motion. I knew the sound all too well, and it looked like there was information missing from the murder board.

VICTIM

Darlene Nichols
Alcoholic?
Jealous
Angry
A wild card
Didn't get along with aunt
Engaged to cheater

SUSPECTS
Ellie (Cousin)
Works Corked
Mom accused of embezzlement
Upset about victim's death
Upset prior to discovery of body.
NO ALIBI

Rhonda Nichols
Gold-digger?
Disliked victim
Husband died recently
Inherited everything
Possible affair with COP
NO ALIBI

Paul Nichols
Jealous and greedy
Narcissist
Was angry with sister

NO ALIBI

<u>*Donna Patterson*</u>
Disliked victim
NO ALIBI

<u>*Blake Perkins*</u>
Fiancé of victim
Cheater
Homophobic idiot
Drunk
Mediocre singer/ talent
NO ALIBI

The last line on Blake's about his talent had been Tippi's idea. She thought it would hurt more than all the others put together. Devious minx.

Under Donna's name, I added,

tried to poison customers at restaurant
     sleeping with brother of victim

"You're crazy," Donna accused. "Me and Paul? I can't stand him and he can't stand me."

"So, you'd like everyone to believe." I fixed my gaze on Ellie. "Is it true your cousin shared everything with you? Sometimes even boys?"

Ellie blushed, her pale cheeks turning a mottled red. "Yes."

"Did she confide in you about what she saw in the wine cellar at Corked?"

Ellie's lower lip began to quiver. "Yeh...yes."

"Well?" I urged.

"She found Paul and Donna half naked and a shattered bottle of Port on the floor. They threatened her that if she told anyone, she'd pay for it." Ellie began to sob.

"This is ridiculous!" Paul said. "I don't have to sit here for this." He tried to stand up, but Copper placed a hand on his shoulder and shoved him back down.

Donna looked a little green, but she didn't say anything to defend herself.

"Donna," Rhonda said. "Tell them this isn't true."

Shut up!" Donna snapped. "If you hadn't moved us here, away from our whole life, none of this would be happening."

I resisted the urge to rub my hands together like an evil mastermind. The suspects were talking, and better yet, they were starting to turn on each other. My plan was starting to come together.

"Blake." I pointed a finger of accusation at him. "You're a jerk, but you aren't a killer."

He let out a blustery breath that wreaked of booze, then sobbed, "It's true. It's all true. I'm a jerk. Darlene deserved so much better from me. I didn't kill her, but she might still be alive if I hadn't been such a terrible man."

I threw up a mental block for my visions just in case I

got a mind full of memories about Blake and his stinky breath. "Thank you for your candor."

Ellie's expression was sympathetic as she stared at Blake, but there was something else there as well.

Cripes. Sometimes even boys.

"Moving on." I looked over at Ezra to see if I was piling it on too thick, but he gave me a nod of encouragement. "Ellie," I said, "you're sweet and a little daft. I'm sure you and Blake will make pretty babies, but you are not a killer."

She clutched her chest and slumped down in her chair with relief.

I might've been generous when I said she was only a little daft. Stupid would have been a better word, but it was mean. I wasn't mean.

"Now it's Donna's turn. You have been sleeping with the enemy." I hadn't had much information about Donna, just a gut feeling but no memories, so I was surprised when she confessed on her own.

"It's all Paul! I didn't want to go along with any of it. He has been sabotaging the vineyards since before Tommy died. I helped him, but only because he made me!"

I recognized the high-pitched whine as she put all the blame on Paul. "You tried to poison the food with rotten meat."

Rhonda's eyes widened. "You did what?"

"I didn't do anything!" Donna said. "I couldn't."

"You are useless," Paul spat. "Worse than useless."

Now Donna was crying as well. "I think we're going to need some tissue," I informed the nearest officer.

"Can we get on with this?" Paul said. "I'm not going to confess to anything, because I haven't done anything, and you have no evidence to prove otherwise."

"Au contraire, mon frere. Or in this case, the victim's brother," I said. "I do have evidence. And do you know why?"

He glowered at me.

"Because your sister wasn't as helpless at the end as you thought. You hit her on the head with that wine bottle, and then you left to go get Rhonda's corkscrew from the bar. But what you don't know is that your sister had taken something from you.

"Something that she managed to hide before your return. She also left us a clue about where she was killed by scratching a chip out of the bottle rack in this restaurant's wine cellar." I said the last part with a lot of dramatics.

I waved Copper over. He had an evidence bag in his hand that he held out for Paul to see.

"Exhibit A," I said, copying something I'd seen on a lawyer drama. "Your Alpha Zeta pin. She snatched it off your collar when she fought you and held it even after you bludgeoned her. She was strong, Paul. Stronger than you."

Paul's fists were clenched so tight his knuckles had gone white.

In an angry, drunken stupor, Blake launched himself

in Paul's direction. Two uniforms grappled him to the ground before he got very far.

I rounded on Paul. "You put on rain gear to keep her blood off you, then choked her with one hand while you killed her with the corkscrew." The one-hand choke was based on what Copper had told me. It was a guess, but I was mostly sure I was right.

"You're out of your mind," the man said.

I still didn't know how he froze her body, but an idea crossed my mind. I walked closer to Paul. Ezra and Copper moved with me, neither of them trusting the man.

"It was cold," I said. "So very cold. You can smell the chill, the ozone, the ice burn." I was trying to elicit a scent memory without the scent. If he thought about how it smelled, maybe I could find out what happened after the cellar.

Paul's Adam's apple bobbed as he nervously swallowed. "I don't know what you're talking about."

"Your sister's face turning blue as you stuffed her in the..."

"Cripes, you need to lose weight," a man says. He's tall and thin, wearing a gray rain suit. The hood is down. He stuffs bloody gloves into his pocket as he finishes the job. "I just need to keep you on ice for a little while."

I recognize the room. It's right after the grape crushers. He dumps Darlene into a wine vat before running the glycol chiller at the winery to super-cool the temperature. He takes

169

some hair from a brush and tucks it into her hand before squeezing her fingers tight around it.

"It won't be long, and I'll finally be free. And soon, I'll have everything I deserve.

No truer words have ever been spoken.

"He froze her with the glycol chiller," I told Chief Porter. "I bet you will find her DNA inside the machine. And he wasn't wearing gloves when he adjusted the temperature on the unit."

"You can't know that." Paul's stare was wide and scared. "You can't know."

"But she does!" Tippi chirped in. I gave her a sideways glance, and she held her hand up apologetically. "Sorry. Got caught up in the moment. My bad."

I glared at the vicious vintner. "As Tippi said, I do know. I know everything, Paul. You took her out to the field before nine in the morning. It must've rained when you brought the corkscrew back with you because you left puddles on the winery floor.

"Framing Rhonda, well, you were just killing two birds with one stone. Darlene believed you when you told her that you had proof that your uncle's will was faked, and she wouldn't let up. Then she found out about your affair with Donna, and all hell was getting ready to rain down on you." Most of this was a guess, but his expression told me I'd nailed it.

"She was your sister, man!" Blake coughed a sob. "Your sister. What the hell is wrong with you?"

Paul rose to his feet, and three police officers

approached him. He rolled his neck and then pinned Rhonda with a withering glare. "I hope you rot in Hell."

She answered his taunt. "And I hope you rot in jail."

As they put the cuffs on Paul and read him his rights, Gilly came over and, with an old man's voice, whispered, "And I would've gotten away with it too if it hadn't been for you meddling kids."

I gave her a grateful smile. "I'm sorry your fun got spoiled."

"Are you kidding? This is a bachelorette to end all bachelorettes. It's the stuff of legends." She hugged me. "Just like you, my friend."

When Gilly left, Ezra came up behind me and said, "That was super-hot."

"Not too much?"

"No, baby. It was just right."

Chief Porter gave his men instructions, including appointing Copper to take the lead on Paul's investigation. There would be blood in the cellar, and I bet they'd also find it in the vat. Paul would be lucky to see daylight ever again once they secured a conviction. Finally, he told Ellie and Donna they could leave but to make themselves available for questioning.

When the chief was finished, he walked over and shook my hand. "Don't take this the wrong way, Ms. Black, but I'd like it very much if you left my town and didn't return. Ever."

I laughed and shook my head. I nodded toward Rhonda. "Life's too short, Chief. Go find joy."

Rhonda's surprised intake of breath wasn't surprising to me at all. She slowly stood and approached the man who brought her joy. I hoped through all the sadness they *would* find joy, but that wasn't my problem or my business.

Lastly, we talked to Copper. "Thank you, Nora and Ezra. I appreciate your help and your discretion."

"It was our privilege," I told the young officer. "You're a good policeman. Smart, and you know when to push back. Keep it up, and one day you'll be chief."

Ezra nodded his agreement. "And, if you ever want to go even further, look me up in Garden Cove. I think you'd make a fine detective. You have good instincts."

Copper grinned as he shook Ezra's hand. "Don't be surprised if I show up one day and take you up on the offer."

"I hope you do," Ezra said sincerely. "I really do."

Gilly and Scott had put their heads together with the rest of our crew by the front entrance. I leaned against Ezra, thoroughly weary after my performance. "Take me home, sweetheart. Let's get Gilly hitched."

"For you, anything."

"You prove it every day."

"And I'll never stop." He slipped his hand into mine, and our fingers intertwined. "Let's go home."

CHAPTER

EIGHTEEN

S *aturday, Gilly's big day...we made it!*

Gilly's gown was blue and cream with gold accents. A classic A-line that hugged her curves with off-the-shoulder sleeves. Her hair was piled in a classy, loose bun, making her look as if Venus herself had decided to live among the mortals.

In other words, my best friend for life was stunningly beautiful. "Scott hit the jackpot. You deserve all the happiness in the world, and I want you to have everything you've ever dreamed up, Gillian Judith Martin. You are a freaking catch and don't you ever forget it."

Gilly's brown eyes glistened. "Don't make me cry, Nora. I just got my makeup perfect." She dipped her forehead to mine. "Thank you."

"For what?"

"For loving me. For loving my kids. For never judging

me, even when I made some of the biggest bonehead moves."

"Firstly, I judge you all the time."

"Nora!" She punched my shoulder, and we laughed.

"I'm teasing. You're very easy to love. Your kids are definitely easy to love. And you never judge *me*. I'm led by your example. Besides, most of the bonehead moves came from a place of incredible bravery. You've never been afraid to seek happiness. I respect the hell out of you for that. You are an inspiration."

"Now, you've ruined my makeup!" she chuckled as tears fell from her eyes. "What would I have ever done without you."

"You won't have to find out because, even if I die, I'll be back to haunt your butt."

She nodded as she dabbed at the corner of her eyes. "Ditto that. Only, how about if we both live?"

There was a knock at the bedroom door, and Pippa stuck her head inside. "T minus ten minutes," she said. "The house is gorgeous. Ari and Marco are waiting for you at the bottom of the stairs to walk you down the aisle."

The aisle was Gilly's backyard. Scott had paid decorators to transform the house and the backyard into a wedding fantasy. Lavender wisteria, white roses, blue orchids, and cream lilies were used liberally, along with fairy lights woven throughout. Our backyards were next to each other. I'd given the decorator permission to place the big reception canopy, decorated just as immaculately, on my side.

Pippa's eyes misted. "It should be illegal to be that gorgeous."

"Stop it. Between you and Nora, I'm not going to make it out of here with any eyeliner left."

Pippa laughed. "You about ready?"

Gilly nodded, then waved her in. "Come sit."

Pippa's dress was the same color blue as Tippi's and mine. Only mine had gold accents to denote me as the maid of honor.

Gilly took out two boxes, one blue and one cream, both neatly decorated with gold bows. "I have gifts for you."

"Gilly!" I protested. "Today is all about you."

"You guys are a part of me, so it's not cheating."

Pippa, thankfully, was having a good day. Scott had advised her to take a multivitamin with B-complex and folic acid until she could see her physician for more tests. Tippi and I had driven her to the pharmacy to ensure she got the supplements and started taking them.

Truthfully, Pippa seemed to be doing better. She hadn't complained about feeling overly tired all day. Her renewed energy could've been the adrenaline related to Gilly's wedding, but I hope the fix for her symptoms was this simple.

She took a seat to the left of Gilly's makeup vanity. Gilly handed me the blue box and Pippa the cream. "I gave Tippi her gift earlier, so go ahead," she said. "Open them."

I took the top off mine. Inside was a two-inch rose quartz heart and a note that said, Thank you for your unconditional love.

"I love it," I told her. "It's perfect."

Pippa opened hers next, and she let out a soft gasp. "A pregnancy test?"

My eyes went wide. "I'm glad that was your box."

Gilly snickered. "You've been walking around tired, moody, and occasionally sick to your stomach. I was that way for the first month of my pregnancy with the twins. Some days I would sleep for fifteen hours. So, instead of getting all freaked out about a doom-and-gloom diagnosis, let's rule out another baby. And there's an amethyst crystal in the box as well for serenity and trust."

"Pregnant?" Pippa questioned, stunned. "It can't be. I don't feel anything like I did when I was pregnant with J.J., and I had a period last month."

"Sometimes people spot when they're pregnant," Gilly said. "I did the first couple months with the twins."

Pippa eyes were bewildered. "Do you really think I might be?"

"Well, now you can find out," Gilly said. She took our hands. "Come on, girls. I'm ready."

We walked Gilly carefully down the staircase and handed her off to Marco and Ari. They both wore tuxedos. Marcos was black with a gold bow tie and cummerbund, while Ari's was cream with a blue bow tie, no cummerbund.

The room was scented with jasmine and wisteria. Pippa and I grabbed our bouquets from the flower table and walked toward the back door.

"Hold on one minute," Pippa said to me. "I'll be right back."

"You have two minutes," I hissed. At seven sharp, they were starting this wedding with or without her. I peered out at the guests. All the seats were filled with Gilly and Scott's friends and loved ones. Tippi, who had J.J. in hand, went to the door. "J.J. is the reluctant flower girl. Every time I try to send her down, she runs back into the house."

I couldn't squat in the dress, so I bent over as far as I could, to get on J.J.'s level. The toddler, with her mother's fine bone features and her father's dark hair, grinned at me.

"Nant-Nora," she mouthed.

"Hello, Judith Jean. Are you behaving for your aunt Tippi?"

"No," the toddler declared, and I couldn't help but laugh.

Jordy, dressed in a gray suit, came to rescue his daughter. "I'll walk down with her."

Tippi smiled. "Thank you! It's hard to wrangle a two, nearly two-and-a-half-year-old when wearing a tight dress." A couple of minutes passed, and the music started. Tippi's brow creased with worry. "Where's Pippa?"

"She'll be here," I said. "Go on. We're right behind you, just like the rehearsal." At least, I hoped so."

One, two, three, four... Pippa had until five to get in position.

"I'm here!" Pippa said, hustling as fast as the dress would allow.

"You okay?" I asked.

She dipped her fingers into her bouquet and extracted the pregnancy test. There was a big pink plus sign right in the stick's center.

A woosh of relief filled me. Pippa wasn't dying. "That's wonderful."

She put the stick back into the bouquet and put her finger up. "Shhh. Our secret until after the reception. Nothing is going to take the focus from Gilly tonight."

I squeezed her hand, then let go as she started down the aisle.

I was next, and I found myself smiling so hard that my cheeks hurt. Ezra was standing with Jordy, who was now holding J.J., and Scott's younger brother, Adam, a med student from Kansas City, was the best man. They were all so handsome.

When I got into the position nearest to where the bride would stand, the wedding march began to play.

Like a Hollywood starlet, Gilly stepped out onto the back patio with her twins on either side, and the guests murmured their appreciation as she sashayed down the aisle.

Her gaze was glued to Scott's, and I swear the man looked like he would pass out from pure bliss. Gilly had love, honest and true. The kind that endures, and I couldn't wait to watch it grow.

THE END...FOR now.

PIT PERFECT MURDER

BARKSIDE OF THE MOON COZY MYSTERIES
BOOK 1

Chapter 1 - Sneak Peek

When I was eighteen years old, I came home from a sleepover and found my mom and dad with their throats cut, and their hearts ripped from their chests.

My little brother Danny was in a broom closet in the kitchen, his arms wrapped around his knees, and his face pale and ghostly. Until that day, I'd planned to go to college and study medicine after graduation, but instead, I ended up staying home and taking care of my seven-year-old brother.

Seventeen years later, my brother was murdered. At the time, Danny's death looked like it would go unsolved, much like my parents' had.

Without Haze Kinsey, my best friend since we were five, the killers would have gotten away with it. She was a special agent for the FBI for almost a decade, and when I called her about Danny's death, she dropped everything to come help me get him justice. The evil group of witches and Shifters responsible for the decimation of my family paid with their lives.

Yes. I said witches and Shifters. Did I forget to mention I'm a werecougar? Oh, and my friend Hazel is a witch. Recently, I discovered witches in my own family tree on my mother's side. Shifters, in general, only mated with Shifters, but witches were the exception. As a matter of fact, my friend Haze is mated to a bear Shifter.

I wouldn't have known about the witch in my genealogy, though, if a rogue witch coven hadn't done some funky hoodoo witchery to me. Apparently, the spell activated a latent talent that had been dormant in my hybrid genes.

My ancestor's magic acted like truth serum to anyone who came near her. No one could lie in her presence. Lucky me, my ability was a much lesser form of hers. People didn't have to tell me the truth, but whenever they were around me, they had the compulsion to overshare all sorts of private matters about themselves. This can get seriously uncomfortable for all parties involved. Like, the fact that I didn't need to know that Janet Strickland had been wearing the same pair of underwear for an entire week, or that Mike Dandridge had sexual fantasies about clowns.

My newfound talent made me unpopular and unwelcome in a town full of paranormal creatures who thrived on little deceptions. So, when Haze discovered the whereabouts of my dad's brother, a guy I hadn't known even existed, I sold all my belongings, let the bank have my parents' house, jumped in my truck, and headed south.

After two days and 700 miles of nonstop gray, snowy weather, I pulled my screeching green and yellow mini-truck into an auto repair shop called The Rusty Wrench. Much like my beloved pickup, I'd needed a new start, and moving to a small town occupied by humans seemed the best shot. I'd barely made it to Moonrise, Missouri before my truck began its death throes. The vehicle protested the last 127 miles by sputtering to a halt as I rolled her into the closest spot.

The shop was a small white-brick building with a one-car garage off to the right side. A black SUV and a white compact car occupied two of the six parking spots.

A sign on the office door said: *No Credit Cards. Cash Only. Some Local Checks Accepted (Except from Earl—You Know Why, Earl! You check-bouncing bastard).*

A man in stained coveralls, wiping a greasy tool with a rag, came out the side door of the garage. He had a full head of wavy gray hair, bushy eyebrows over light blue, almost colorless eyes, and a minimally lined face that made me wonder about his age. I got out of the truck to greet him.

"Can I help you, miss?" His voice was soft and raspy with a strong accent that was not quite Deep South.

"Yes, please." I adjusted my puffy winter coat. "The

heater stopped working first. Then the truck started jerking for the last fifty miles or so."

He scratched his stubbly chin. "You could have thrown a rod, sheared the distributor, or you have a bad ignition module. That's pretty common on these trucks."

I blinked at him. I could name every muscle in the human body and twelve different kinds of viruses, but I didn't know a spark plug from a radiator cap. "And that all means..."

"If you threw a rod, the engine is toast. You'll need a new vehicle."

"Crap." I grimaced. "What if it's the other thingies?"

The scruffy mechanic shrugged. "A sheared distributor is an easy fix, but I have to order in the part, which means it won't get fixed for a couple of days. Best-case scenario, it's the ignition module. I have a few on hand. Could get you going in a couple of hours, but..." he looked over my shoulder at the truck and shook his head, "...I wouldn't get your hopes up."

I must've looked really forlorn because the guy said, "It might not need any parts. Let me take a look at it first. You can grab a cup of coffee across the street at Langdon's One-Stop."

He pointed to the gas station across the road. It didn't look like much. The pale-blue paint on the front of the building looked in need of a new coat, and the weather-beaten sign with the store's name on it had seen better days. There was a car at the gas pumps and a couple more in the parking lot, but not enough to call it busy.

I'd had enough of one-stops, though, thank you. The bathrooms had been horrible enough to make a wereraccoon yark, and it took a lot to make those garbage eaters sick. Besides, I wasn't just passing through Moonrise, Missouri.

"Have you ever heard of The Cat's Meow Café?" Saying the name out loud made me smile the way it had when Hazel had first said it to me. I'd followed my GPS into town, so I knew I wasn't too far away from the place.

"Just up the street about two blocks, take a right on Sterling Street. You can't miss it. I should have some news in about an hour or so, but take your time."

"Thank you, Mister..."

"Greer." He shoved the tool in his pocket. "Greer Knowles."

"I'm Lily Mason."

"Nice to meet ya," said Greer. "The place gets hoppin' around noon. That's when church lets out."

I looked at my phone. It was a little before noon now. "Good. I could go for something to eat. How are the burgers?"

"Best in town," he quipped.

I laughed. "Good enough."

Even in the sub-freezing temperature, my hands were sweating in my mittens. I wasn't sure what had me more nervous, leaving the town I grew up in for the first time in my life or meeting an uncle I'd never known existed.

I crossed a four-way intersection. One of the signs was missing, and I saw the four-by-four post had snapped off at its base. I hadn't noticed it on my way in. Crap. Had I run a stop sign? I walked the two blocks to Sterling. The diner was just where Greer had said. A blue truck, a green mini-coup, and a sheriff's SUV were parked out front.

An alarm dinged as the glass door opened to The Cat's Meow. Inside, there was a row of six booths along the wall, four tables that seated four out in the open floor, and counter seating with about eight cushioned black stools. The interior décor was rustic country with orange tabby kitsch everywhere. A man in blue jeans and a button-down shirt with a string tie sat in the nearest booth. A female police officer sat at a counter chair sipping coffee and eating a cinnamon roll. Two elderly women, one with snowball-white hair, the other a dyed strawberry-blonde, sat in a back booth.

The white poof-headed lady said, "This egg is not over-medium."

"Well, call the mayor," said Redhead. "You're unhappy with your eggs. Again."

"See this?" She pointed at the offending egg. "Slime, right here. Egg snot. You want to eat it?"

"If it'll make you shut up about breakfast food, I'll eat it and lick the plate."

A man with copper-colored hair and a thick beard,

tall and well-muscled, stepped out of the kitchen. He wore a white apron around his waist, and he had on a black T-shirt and blue jeans. He held a plate with a single fried egg shining in the middle.

The old woman with the snowy hair blushed, her thin skin pinking up as he crossed the room to their table. "Here you go, Opal. Sorry 'bout the mix-up on your egg." He slid the plate in front of her. "This one is pure perfection." He grinned, his broad smile shining. "Just like you." He winked.

Opal giggled.

The redhead rolled her eyes. "You're as easy as the eggs."

"Oh, Pearl. You're just mad he didn't flirt with you."

As the women bickered over the definition of flirting, the cook glanced at me. He seemed startled to see me there. "You can sit anywhere," he said. "Just pick an open spot."

"I'm actually looking for someone," I told him.

"Who?"

"Daniel Mason." Saying his name gave me a hollow ache. My parents had named my brother Daniel, which told me my dad had loved his brother, even if he didn't speak about him.

The man's brows rose. "And why are you looking for him?"

I immediately knew he was a werecougar like me. The scent was the first clue, and his eyes glowing, just for a second, was another. "You're Daniel Mason, aren't you?"

He moved in closer to me and whispered barely audibly, but with my Shifter senses, I heard him loud and clear. "I go by Buzz these days."

"Who's your new friend, Buzz?" the policewoman asked. Now that she was looking up from her newspaper, I could see she was young.

He flashed a charming smile her way. "Never you mind, Nadine." He gestured to a waitress, a middle-aged woman with sandy-colored hair, wearing a black T-shirt and a blue jean skirt. "Top off her coffee, Freda. Get Nadine's mind on something other than me."

"That'll be a tough 'un, Buzz." Freda laughed. "I don't think Deputy Booth comes here for the cooking."

"More like the cook," the elderly lady with the light strawberry-blonde hair said. She and her friend cackled.

The policewoman's cheeks turned a shade of crimson that flattered her chestnut-brown hair and pale complexion. "Y'all mind your P's and Q's."

Buzz chuckled and shook his head. He turned his attention back to me. "Why is a pretty young thing like you interested in plain ol' me?"

I detected a slight apprehension in his voice.

"If you're Buzz Mason, I'm Lily Mason, and you're my uncle."

The man narrowed his dark-emerald gaze at me. "I think we'd better talk in private."

Keep Reading!

PARANORMAL MYSTERIES & ROMANCES
BY RENEE GEORGE

Nora Black Midlife Psychic Mysteries

Sense & Scent Ability (Book 1)

For Whom the Smell Tolls (Book 2)

War of the Noses (Book 3)

Aroma With A View (Book 4)

Spice and Prejudice (Book 5)

Age of Inno-Scents (Book 6)

Aroma Holiday (Book 7)

The Vapes of Wrath (Book 8)

Grimoires of a Middle-aged Witch

Earth Spells Are Easy (Book 1)

Spell On Fire (Book 2)

When the Spells Blows (Book 3)

Spell Over Troubled Water (Book 4)

Ghost in the Spell (Book 5)

Peculiar Mysteries & Romances

You've Got Tail (Book 1)

My Furry Valentine (Book 2)

Thank You For Not Shifting (Book 3)

My Hairy Halloween (Book 4)

In the Midnight Howl (Book 5)

Furred Lines (Book 6)

My Wolfy Wedding (Book 7)

Who Let The Wolves Out? (Book 8)

My Thanksgiving Faux Paw (Book 9)

Witchin' Impossible Paranormal Mysteries

Witchin' Impossible (Book 1)

Rogue Coven (Book 2)

Familiar Protocol (Booke 3)

Mr & Mrs. Shift (Book 4)

Barkside of the Moon Paranormal Mysteries

Pit Perfect Murder (Book 1)

Murder & The Money Pit (Book 2)

The Pit List Murders (Book 3)

Pit & Miss Murder (Book 4)

The Prune Pit Murder (Book 5)

Two Pits and A Little Murder (Book 6)

Pits and Pieces of Murder (Book 7)

Pittie Party Murder (Book 8)

Hex Drive

Hex Me, Baby, One More Time (Book 1)

Oops, I Hexed It Again (Book 2)

I Want Your Hex (Book 3)

Hex Me With Your Best Shot (Book 4)

Hex Me All Night Long (Book 5)

Madder Than Hell

Gone With The Minion (Book 1)

Devil On A Hot Tin Roof (Book 2)

A Street Car Named Demonic (Book 3)

ABOUT THE AUTHOR

I am a USA Today Bestselling author who writes paranormal mysteries and romances because I love all things whodunit, Otherworldly, and weird. Also, I wish my pittie, the adorable Kona Princess Warrior and my two cats Ash and Simon could talk. Or at least be more like Scooby-Doo and help me unmask villains at the haunted house up the street.

When I'm not writing about mystery-solving were-cougars or the adventures of a hapless psychic living among shapeshifters, I am preyed upon by stray kittens who end up living in my house because I can't say no to those sweet, furry faces. (Someone stop telling them where I live!)

I live in Mid-Missouri with my family and I spend my non-writing time doing really cool stuff...like watching TV and cleaning up dog poop

Follow Renee!
Bookbub
Renee's Rebel Readers FB Group
Newsletter